HARD LINE

HARD LINE

Michael Z. Lewin

A Foul Play Press Book

The Countryman Press, Inc.
Woodstock, Vermont

This edition published in 1996 by Foul Play Press,
a division of The Countryman Press, Inc.,
Woodstock, Vermont

ISBN 0-88150-346-0

10 9 8 7 6 5 4 3 2 1

Cover design © 1996 by Honi Werner

Printed in Canada

1

The telephone rang.

Powder looked at his watch. He let the phone ring twice more. Then he rubbed his face with one hand, and picked up the receiver with the other.

Because it was twenty minutes till the office opened, he didn't say, "Missing Persons." He said, "E one forty-four."

"Is Roy Powder there, please?" A man at the other end, being familiar.

"This is Powder."

"Cedric Kendall, County Hospital, Roy."

Powder relaxed. "How do, Cedric."

"You are almost the only person in Indianapolis I can count on to be at work before he's supposed to," Kendall said amicably. One hardworking administrator to another.

"No," Powder said. "I've just got a new sergeant coming in today, so I was clearing part of the work load in order to have a little instruction time."

"Your people don't seem to last very long with you," Kendall noted. "Or is this one in addition to the ones you already have?"

"Don't get me started," Powder said. "There are more politics here than in Washington."

"I see."

"So, what you got for me? A body needs identifying?"

"Yes and sort of."

"Elucidate," Powder said.

Powder picked up a pencil and rubbed gently on his lower lip.

"Two problems came in overnıght. One *is* an unidentified deceased. Elderly male. Exposure, possibly. Alcohol poisoning, possibly. We're cutting him up this afternoon."

"OK," Powder said.

"And the other is an unidentified live person."

"Makes a change."

"Female. Young, perhaps in her late twenties."

"Unconscious?"

"No," Kendall said portentously. "Conscious but seeming to suffer from amnesia."

"Oh," Powder said.

"Two guys found her in an alley last night. They were on their way home from a bar. Sam's on Trowbridge Street, near Hoyt. Do you know it?"

"I've passed it," Powder said. "What time of night was this?"

"About one this morning," Kendall said. "According to the report I've got."

"Police report?"

"No. Ambulance."

Powder hesitated. "Do I detect from your voice that there is more?"

"For a start, she was stark-naked when they found her."

"I see," Powder said quietly.

"What the two guys told the ambulance man is that they wouldn't have noticed her but for the fire."

"Fire?"

"She was burning her clothes. Back from the road.

Apparently the alley turns and she was at the bend. They spotted the light and went to look. She saw them coming and . . ." He held the conclusion for a moment.

Powder bit. "And what?"

"And she took her gun . . ."

"Jesus Christ. A nice class of patient you people get over there."

"And she put it in her mouth and she pulled the trigger."

"What happened? No bullet?"

"There was a bullet all right. But the gun misfired. Cheapo twenty-two. Then they got to her and pulled the gun out. It brought a couple of teeth with it and she was choking on the blood. They took her back to the bar and called the ambulance."

Powder thought for a moment. "The bar was open?"

"One of them owns it."

"When did the ambulance get there?"

"Quarter to two."

"Who has the gun?"

"We do. It's locked away."

"And that pile of clothes?"

"I don't know."

"How about the details for the guys who found her?"

"I've got two names here."

Powder took the names.

"I'll check the Night Cover log," he said. "And if they don't know anything about it upstairs, then maybe I'll be around. But it won't be for a while yet."

The Missing Persons Department's part-time secretary came in the private door at two minutes to nine. She was a gangly woman of twenty-two, a civilian, who worked mornings for the police in order to pay for afternoons in computer technology. How, exactly, her classes fitted with her employment Powder didn't know. But she'd been at it for nine months. And Powder did know that she flew through the routine paperwork, to be able to spend time punching away at the keys of the computer terminal in the department office, which connected to the central IPD computer.

"Morning, Lieutenant," Agnes Shorter said cheerfully as she came in. When on her feet, she was active and chatty. When she sat down she became quiet and precise.

"Agnes," Powder said, by way of acknowledgment.

Shorter sat immediately at the terminal desk and began to type on the keyboard. Then stopped. "Rats," she said. "Somebody's using what I want."

Powder didn't ask what that might be. He said, "I'm going to have to go out."

"All right."

"This Sergeant Fleetwood is supposed to be here . . ." He looked at his watch. ". . . by now, I'd have hoped."

Agnes faced him and smiled.

"I'm going upstairs, but then I'll have to leave the building. You may have to do the initiation ceremonies. Go through our basic routines."

"OK, Lieutenant."

Powder rose.

Agnes turned back to the keyboard and played a few chords.

Powder used the stairs for the trip from first floor to fourth. Using stairs was part of his diet and had almost become habit.

On the fourth, he went to the detective dayroom and checked the records for the previous night. A phone call from the ambulance service had been logged, but no file opened and no case assigned.

For the sake of formality, he noted that he was making

a follow-up investigation. But he doubted that anyone would notice his notes. These days Night Cover records were treated as having the same permanency as daily newspapers. They were skimmed over in the mornings and that was that.

On the way back to the stairwell Powder passed several officers he had worked with in the past. He exchanged no more acknowledgment with any of them than a nod.

The stairs were empty.

Rather than use the back door, for Missing Persons personnel, Powder came into the department through the public entrance. Agnes looked up momentarily, but continued with her work.

Powder fussed for a moment with the chairs facing a rubber plant on the right side of the entrance. In the corner of the room behind the chairs a basket of variegated ivies and philodendrons hung from midway up the wall.

The main Missing Persons counter faced the door, with only one small section at the end made semiprivate by a fan-shaped barrier at right angles to the counter top. But genuinely private interviews could only take place in a small room just inside the main door on the left.

For Powder there were two ways from the front of the counter to the back. One was through the interview room, which had a connecting door for department officers. The other was through a flap in the counter top.

"Excuse me, please."

Behind Powder a woman in a bulky wheelchair, with two aluminum stick crutches holstered behind the seat like a pair of flags, was asking to get past.

"Will you get out of my way please?" the woman said again, when Powder did not immediately make way. "You may have time to stand around, but I have things to do."

Powder frowned and continued to block the wheelchair's path. "They told me," he said measuredly, "that you would be out of that thing and walking around."

The woman blinked. She sat back and looked up at him. "Which means that you must be Lieutenant Powder," she said.

Powder's frown grew easily into a scowl.

"And you are the kid who thinks that she can do with half a body what most of us have a hard time doing with a whole one."

Sergeant Fleetwood had a choice of provocations to respond to. She said, "Hardly a child."

"How old?"

"Twenty-eight."

"Fifty-three percent of the people in this country are older than you."

"And seven months."

"Roll in," Powder said. "I won't ask you to take a seat."

Fleetwood followed Powder through the gap in the counter. Powder gallantly held the flap up for her.

"Not exactly Five Hundred standard with that thing, are you?"

"I'll be out of it full-time soon."

"And onto the crutches?"

"For a while."

"Terrific, kid. Terrific."

"I'm glad you think so too, Lieutenant."

"Generally," he said, "we use the back door here. If you think you can handle it."

"I'll find some knobs to practice on."

"Agnes over there will give you a key."

At the mention of her name, Agnes glanced up from the computer keyboard and appeared only just to have noticed Powder and Fleetwood so near to her.

Agnes said, "Hi."

Fleetwood said, "Hello, Agnes; Carollee Fleetwood."

Powder rubbed his face and glowered down at his new sergeant. "This isn't a soft billet," he said.

"Now why would I think that?" Fleetwood asked. "Certainly not because the Missing Persons Department is tucked downstairs into a corner of what used to be Traffic Fines space, or because it closes for lunch, or because it's across the hall from the public toilets. Surely I'm not so small-minded as to suggest that it is anything but the very heart of the Indianapolis Police Department's investigative arm."

Despite himself, Powder broke into a smile. "You forgot the chaplain. Right across the hall from the goddamn chaplain."

It could have been received as an offer of truce.

But Fleetwood said, "That must be handy when you need consoling."

Powder stopped smiling. He said, "I hear he does a special line in cripples."

"We're not 'crippled' anymore. We're 'disabled' now."

"Great. And while we're chatting, let me say that if you haven't got your head sorted out any better than your mode of transportation, and if you're going to be crying into your hanky all day long because you can't run around chasing bank robbers anymore, then maybe you better take your tricycle and get out now."

"Thank you for that warm welcome."

"I haven't spent five years straightening this department out to end up as a nursemaid."

"I tried to get assigned upstairs," Fleetwood said. Her conciliation?

"It was here or a pension, huh?"

"Just about."

"Terrific, kid. Really great. And do you come with your own baby bottles, or do we have to requisition them?"

"A police wet nurse comes down four times a day and puts the tit to me."

Powder rubbed his face for several seconds. He sat down at his desk and picked up some papers. Then he put them down again.

"What I ask for is two full-time officers. Nothing fancy. Could be kids for me to train up. What they send me is a crippled sergeant. A hypothetical question for you, Sergeant Carollee Fleetwood. If you were in my chair, instead of that one, what would you do?"

"I'd cut the crap and give me a chance."

Powder looked at his watch. "Well, I've enjoyed our little chat, but I've got to run. Agnes will give you a taste of procedures here. And if you find she's ignoring you, pull the plug on that damn machine. She does know how to talk. It's a matter of getting her attention."

"Excuse me, Lieutenant?"

"Yeah?"

"May I ask a few questions?"

"Sure kid, sure. Only not now." Powder left.

2

One end of the alley next to Sam's opened onto Trowbridge Street directly behind the bar. Because the alley ran in a squared-off U shape, its second opening was also on Trowbridge Street, near the other end of the block.

Powder parked in front of the bar. It appeared closed. Instead of trying to raise somebody inside, he walked along the alley. At its first elbow he found the remains of the burned clothes. Shoes, dress, underwear, belt all charred and mixed with cinders as if the fire had been put out by people stomping on it.

Powder photographed the scene from two angles with an instant-print camera. Then he scooped everything in the immediate vicinity into a plastic bag.

Before returning to his car he walked the full length of the alleyway twice, studying the dirt-and-cinder surface, and looking occasionally into the yards of the small houses that backed onto it. Sam's was the only commercial establishment in the immediate area, a brick tavern that had been around since the fifties.

Powder put his plastic bag in the trunk of his car and drove to County Hospital.

* * *

"Hello, Roy," Cedric Kendall said, as Powder entered his office.

"I don't know why you wear that white jacket. Unwary people will mistake you for a doctor."

"It happens sometimes."

Powder looked at the densely booked walls, and at the mass of paper on Kendall's desk. "When was the last time you stuck a knife in somebody?"

Cedric Kendall smiled benignly.

"This morning over breakfast, huh?"

"You can't keep secrets from the police," Kendall said.

"I've come to see your bodies."

"Both?"

"There is no open file on the live one and while I'm here, I'll take prints and a picture of the dead one."

"We take the prints for you," Kendall said. "Part of the routine."

"All yours come in with pressure smudges. I'll do it myself."

Kendall shrugged. He wrote a note and passed it across the desk. "That will get you access to our deceased tenant."

"Guy in the icebox going to be able to read this? Maybe I was wrong. Maybe you are a doctor. It looks just like a prescription."

"And the young lady is in five eleven. I let the head nurse know someone would be coming. Ask for her at the desk in front of the central elevator."

"The patient still without benefit of memory?"

"I didn't ask, Roy. Sorry. But I've made a copy of the ambulance file on her."

"That's the Wishard service?"

"Yes," Kendall said. "They handle virtually all the emergency stuff in the county. And I've got a copy of our admission sheet for you." He handed Powder the two reproductions. And a small .22 automatic pistol.

Powder folded the papers and pocketed them. He handled the gun gingerly. "Cheap and nasty," he said. He put it in another pocket. Then he flipped an imaginary coin, caught it, and turned it on his wrist. "Heads or tails?"

After a momentary double take, Kendall said, "Tails."

"Right. I go see a lady about an identity."

The admission report had very little information on it. The woman was estimated as being in her late twenties, five five, and weighing one thirty. Hair brown, eyes blue. The only distinguishing feature was a well-healed scar at the base of her neck, which, it was speculated, might have been from operations following a broken neck.

Five eleven was a small, spare single room. The woman lay on her side looking at the window, but turned toward the door quickly as Powder entered.

He was startled by the blackness of shock rings around her eyes. But as he pulled up a chair he saw that the eyes inside the targets were alert and suspicious.

"Howdy," Powder said. "How are you feeling this morning?"

"Are you a doctor?" she asked. Her speech was slurred, the mouth swollen.

"Nope. Police. I'm Lieutenant Leroy Powder. This is my ID." He held the card up so she could see it easily. She wasn't interested. "I'm in charge of the city's Missing Persons Department. The hospital has asked me to help find out who you are."

The woman's eyes darted round the room, returning to Powder only intermittently. "I don't know," she said.

"I'd be grateful if you would tell me what you remember?"

"About what?"

"About anything." Complete amicability.

"I remember having some kind of soft cereal for breakfast," she said slowly.

"Did you enjoy it?"

"I don't remember enjoying it or not enjoying it," she said.

Easily, Powder asked, "What's your name?"

The woman looked at him. "I don't remember," she said. Because of the markings and swelling, it was hard to tell what kind of expression was on her face.

"Do you know where you live?"

"No."

"Or where you come from?"

"No."

"Whether you're married?"

"No."

"What happened to give you those scars on the back of your neck?"

A momentary pause. "No."

"Or why you were burning your clothes before you tried to kill yourself?"

Here she clearly reacted and hesitated before saying, "Why what?"

"No one has mentioned that to you?" Powder asked evenly. "You're not a nudist, by any chance?"

The woman squinted, wagged her head again, and said, "I don't think so."

Powder tipped back onto the back legs of the molded plastic chair. "Naked as a jaybird," he said. "Chanting a mystical song and praying for rain until two people you'd waked up with the howling and racket—"

The woman shook her head again, and lay back onto the pillows behind her.

"A young couple," Powder said, "disturbed by the

merriment, came down to see what was happening and no sooner did they appear in the alleyway than you picked up a gun and took a couple of pot shots at them." Powder drew the automatic from his pocket and raised it, at arm's length, to point at the woman's face.

"No," the woman said, beginning a response but ending with a strangled sound.

"Excuse?" Powder said. "I didn't quite hear."

"I didn't say anything. Nothing."

"Except to deny my version of the story," Powder said. He let the chair come forward onto all four legs again, then leaned closer to the woman, who had turned her face away. "It doesn't much matter anyway," he said. "I came here not believing that you have amnesia."

She said nothing.

He pulled his chair up to the edge of her bed. "I'm fifty-three. I've only got seven toes and my remaining hair is so gray people are always surprised that I'm not in a wheelchair. I've known a lot of people who think their troubles are insupportable. Once they decide to cut the crap, they find there are good things along with the bad. So give it a think and I'll be back with my notebook tomorrow."

The head nurse on the fifth floor, a slightly built woman with large, commanding eyes and an aura of authority, called Powder over as he waited by the elevator.

"How did you do?" she asked him.

"I used my very best bedside manner," he said. "Never fails. Can you tell me the way to your morgue?"

"I want a picture too," Powder told the attendant, after he had taken the fingerprints of the unidentified male corpse. "Help me sit him up a little, will you?"

A series of awkward adjustments allowed Powder to take a face-on shot by standing on a chair.

"Can you get him to smile?"

"If you let me get a chisel."

"Haven't got the time," Powder said. "At least he won't blink. But get your face out of the way, will you? So we can tell which one is dead."

3

*F*leetwood was behind a desk, studying papers. Agnes pounded a typewriter. Powder paused to look at his little family and enjoyed a fleeting sense of satisfaction.

He sat suddenly on Fleetwood's desk top and, as she looked up, he said, "I felt like shooting at a woman just now. There I was, all warm and cozy by her bedside trying to get her to tell me why she took her clothes off, and then I was waving a gun in her face and feeling like sending a couple of shots past her ears to show her I meant business. What do you think of that? I must be losing my mind." He smiled pleasantly and got up.

He went to Agnes's desk and waited until she stopped.

"What have you got for me?" he asked her.

"Two follow-up calls regarding missing juveniles."

"What stage?"

"Both ten-day. And Carollee made a couple of sixties. But there has been no new business. Very quiet. I've been able to go through the whole procedure routine with her."

Powder said, "I've got two new files to open. And there's a set of fingerprints and a gun I want the owners of traced." He passed the fingerprint card and the .22 automatic over to her.

"Prints on the gun?"

"No."

"OK," Agnes said. "I'll take them up as soon as I'm finished here."

Powder returned to Carollee Fleetwood. He pulled up a chair and sat facing her.

"And how is my new sergeant finding life with us?"

"Undemanding," she said.

"Agnes has taken you through the forms and procedures?"

"And gave me this mimeographed booklet. You wrote it, right?"

"It's how I like things done."

"I'll learn it."

"You're right. You will."

Two minutes later, three men entered the office.

Powder looked up and exhaled heavily. The man he knew best was Henry Howard, a sergeant from Public Liaison.

"What do you want, Henry?" Powder asked.

"Good morning, Lieutenant Powder," Howard said with the easy formality of a man about to introduce strangers. "Do you know Ben Brown? *Star* reporter who covers us here?"

"Vaguely," Powder said.

The man referred to nodded, but left the talking to the policeman. The third man carried a camera.

"Well, we've come for a few words and a picture to mark the return to active service of Sergeant Fleetwood. Good to see you again, Carollee."

"Hello, Henry. Ben. Larry."

"Larry is Ben's photographer. Do you think you can come out front, honey?"

Howard lifted the flap to make a passageway for Fleetwood's progress to the public side of the counter. She did not move.

"Get out," Powder said to the men.

"Now look, Lieutenant," Howard said, "I think we all realize that—"

"All three of you. Out." Powder took hold of the flap and slammed it with a frightening noise. "No pictures. No few words."

"News is news. And Sergeant Fleetwood's return to service is good press for the department."

"And for Sergeant Fleetwood. But it is bad press for Missing Persons."

"I think you're overreacting here, Powder."

"Overreacting?" Powder banged his fist on the counter. "*Overreacting?* Who the hell are you to tell me that I'm overreacting because I want my department protected from the curiosity brigade that will march in if you publish a glamour shot of a pretty sergeant showing some dead leg in here?" Powder pounded on the counter top.

Powder raised the flap and charged at the men. "Do a feature for the Sunday magazine about how great a job we do finding juveniles and filtering out the people the detectives don't have time for. About how overworked and understaffed we are, about how well we sniff out suspicious disappearances. Set that up and you can take all the pictures you want."

Howard said, "I'm sure Ben will put that idea to the features people, but in the meantime—"

"In the meantime," Powder said, "you'll take your circus elsewhere. Go upstairs and audition for Miss Police Canteen. A little ice cream and you'll have knee à la mode. But get out of here."

The Public Liaison sergeant turned to the other two men and shrugged. "Sorry guys, but you gather what the lieutenant's attitude is. All I can say is that I'll be reporting it to higher authorities." At the door, Howard turned back to Powder. "You'll be hearing more about this, Lieutenant."

"I'll be dead one day too."

The men left.

Powder rubbed his face.

Agnes, who had been watching the proceedings, returned to the computer terminal keyboard.

Fleetwood sat, motionless, quiet. Watching Powder.

He asked, finally, "How long before you are on those sticks full-time?"

"Soon."

"How long?"

"I don't know how long."

"Why aren't you on them now?"

"My physical control is not quite complete. I'm not reliable enough to use them full-time."

"How long since your misfortune?"

"Six months."

"Uh huh," Powder said. "To the day, by any chance?"

Fleetwood's mouth assumed a wry expression. "I think it may be close, yes."

"So that if you were not on active duty again now, you could be bundled off the force without much ceremony, I believe."

"They will never retire me without a fight."

He nodded slowly. "Papers gave you quite a lot of attention, didn't they?"

"When I was shot," she said, "it did seem that the media were interested."

"A veritable tidal wave of public sympathy, I'd have said. I just hadn't known, before now, how much of it you drummed up for yourself."

"I was under instructions to be cooperative."

Powder continued his acknowledgment, recalling touching television interviews.

"What did the powers-that-be offer when you announced you wanted to come back into service?"

"They wanted me to go to Public Liaison."

"Seems reasonable."

"Screw PR. That's not police work."

"I trust," Powder said, "that you don't think me so stupid as to believe that The Henry, Ben, and Larry Show thought of you all by themselves?"

Fleetwood said nothing.

"No way. No way were they walking down the hall, flicking flies off their noses, thinking, There's Carollee. She's a sport. Let's go take her picture. Do her a good turn. Keep the brass alert to the public interest in her."

He rubbed his face again.

"You've been around now, what, three hours?"

Fleetwood said nothing.

"I am only going to say this once. Your daydreams of walking the streets with seven-shooters on both hips will be dreamed on your own time. Not mine. Not here. I don't give a damn what your long-term ambitions are, and I don't really care how long it is before you can cha-cha-cha. But while you are in this office, hours or years, you will bust ass for Missing Persons and you will build the future career of Carollee Fleetwood on your own time."

Carefully, Fleetwood said, "I read you, Lieutenant Powder. Except that my ass is already busted."

4

*P*owder weakened in front of the desserts. His eyes drifted from cakes to pies. Back to cakes.

"Can we tempt you with something today, Lieutenant?" asked the canteen supervisor, a brisk smiling woman in flowery print dress.

Brought back to awareness of himself, awareness that people paid attention, Powder said, "It should be against the law to sell things like that."

He pushed his pieless tray, with its cottage cheese, yogurt, and whole-meal bread, to the till.

"If you didn't have no temptation, then you'd never have the chance to feel real virtuous, Lieutenant."

Powder picked an empty table on the window side of the small dining area. Facing east and overlooking the Market Square Arena parking lot, the view was less than spectacular, and it was dulled the more because the glass in the window was tinted and very thick. The glass was a relic of the days when the room was the IPD Communications Center, and had to be protected from snipers.

Powder began his lunch with no fear of snipers whatsoever.

Before he had licked his yogurt top, a tall thin man

with a heavily ridged and wrinkled face dropped his tray on the table and slid into the facing chair. "How do, Powder, how do," the man said.

"Tidmarsh," Powder said, by way of acknowledgment. The man was in charge of the department's stored information.

"So," the man said, "how's life with the glamorous heroine?"

Powder looked up. "Who's that?"

"Come off it, Leroy. Everybody in the building knows the raven-haired police beauty, tragically gunned down in the course of duty, the enchanting and ever popular Carollee Fleetwood, fell into your tender mercies today."

"I'm training a new sergeant in Missing Persons procedures, if that's what you mean."

Tidmarsh rocked back in his chair. "I love you, Powder. You crease me."

Powder ate.

"I tried to get her assigned to Computers," Tidmarsh said. "I begged, I pleaded. But they claimed she preferred to work with you."

"Lucky me."

"I suppose it must mean she is innumerate, the poor flower. No one *prefers* to work with you."

"And keep your hands off my computer kid, while you're at it."

"Who's this?" Tidmarsh asked.

"Hired as a secretary but taking courses. She's better than the lot of you and she's staying in Missing Persons."

"How long she been there?"

"Since September."

Tidmarsh said, "I knew some bugger on a terminal had been tying up more free time this year. I should have goddamn known it would be your terminal."

"We need a little computer of our own."

"Sure, sure," Tidmarsh said. "But instead you'll have to make do with Miss Fleetwood."

"Great," Powder said.

"Come off it. Even a bullhead like you has to admire the lady. You wouldn't mind a partner who would step into a slug meant for you. And she had a lot of offers, you know. Outside the force. Even with TV, I hear. With the news, or some damn thing. But she's put her head down and wants to get back to active service. You got to admire that."

"I admire somebody who does the job," Powder said.

Tidmarsh leaned forward. "You figure she's never going to walk again, then?"

"She'll be too fast for you by the Fourth of July," Powder said.

On his way back from lunch Powder stopped at the Forensic Lab on the third floor. There was no reception officer to deal with the range of scientific requests from members of the department, so Powder had to look around for the technician in charge of the lab.

He was bent under a hood that drew away noxious gases.

Powder waited till the man was finished.

Peeling off gloves and mask, the man turned to Powder and greeted him. "Sorry to keep you waiting," the man said. "But once you're in the fart extractor, it's hard to tear yourself away."

"Keeping busy then, Oliver?"

"It's a fulfilling life, forensic science," the man said. He placed a hand over his heart. "I'd recommend it to all little boys and girls. Especially girls."

"I've got something for you."

Oliver peered at the plastic bag Powder carried. "Let me guess. Picnic lunch?"

"A woman's clothes, burned."

"Christ, was she inside them?"

"No."

"As you're in the misplaced-baby section of this police department store," Oliver said, "I presume you wish me to examine these charred remains because you're having trouble making the woman they belonged to."

"In the sense of identifying her, yes," Powder said.

"Is that a glint of ivory I see between those puffy, aged lips? No? Not even a little smile?"

"The owner of the clothes attempted suicide and now doesn't want to be identified. She bothered to try to burn these before she stuck the popgun under her tongue. Maybe she knows better than I do whether they might help tell us who she is."

"OK, Powder. When I get a chance I'll have a look if she left her camp name badge sewn to the inside of her panties."

Fleetwood was alone in the office when Powder returned from Forensic. Her desk was covered with the contents of a lunchbox.

"Agnes gone?" Powder asked.

"About ten minutes ago. She left you some messages."

Powder perused two sheets of paper on the top of an otherwise clean desk surface.

Then he asked. "What do you think you're doing?"

"What do you mean?"

"That stuff."

"My lunch? Is there a problem about that?"

"Several. Count 'em. One, we close for lunch, but if John or Jane Public sees you in here, stuffing your face and making them wait while they're suffering with some loss they hope you are going to fix, it devalues them. It puts them down. We don't do that here."

"Point taken."

"Two, you should get out in the building and mix with the street cops and the detectives as much as you have time for. Find out what's happening with them. Show an interest, and then hit them with what a bastard your boss is and how much it will help you if they happen to notice your Missing Person of the Week that you just happen to have a picture of you can give them."

"Now, wait a—"

"Three, you need all the practice you can get wheeling yourself around."

Fleetwood was silent.

"And four, if you eat here routinely, I will routinely take advantage of you, just like I am going to do now."

Powder took two large manila envelopes from his desk drawers.

"What are you doing?"

"Going out."

"For long?"

"Could be hours," Powder said. "Sink-or-swim time, kid."

5

Powder made a series of routine stops and he also stopped at Sam's, hoping to find the two men who had found the Jane Doe in the alley behind.

One of the men, James Voss, was the owner. He was behind the bar as Powder entered the small, barely lit premises. The darkness fell suddenly as Powder left the bright day. The air conditioner seemed to draw away light as well as warmth. Most of the illumination came from beer brand signs and from the head of a nonelectronic shuttle bowling game.

James Voss didn't look happy. But he looked as if he never looked happy.

Powder identified himself, which did little to cheer Voss up. "You and ..." Powder consulted his notes. "... Andrew Warren found the woman."

"Andy. Yeah. We saw this fire up the alley. Well, a light really. But except for this one, all the buildings around here are wood, so ..."

"It was a long way up the alley."

"We was in no hurry."

"You'd just closed the place?"

"Yeah."

"Busy night?"

Voss, a fat man with rolled-up sleeves, turned to the closest of the bar's four drinkers. "Are any of them busy these days?"

The other man shrugged.

"It was a bright fire?"

"Bright enough to see."

"So you went up the alley."

"Yeah."

"What did you see and hear as you came closer to the fire?"

"Well, I seen the fire and then I seen this woman."

"Standing or sitting?"

"She was standing, looking at the flames."

"Poking it with anything?"

"Nope. She didn't have nothing to poke it with."

"Naked, you told the ambulance men."

"Like a babe," Voss said. "Like a newborn babe."

"Was she that way when you found her?"

"What do you mean?"

"I mean, was she that way when you found her? Or was that only how you left her."

"Look fella. I don't know what the broad has been saying, but we told it absolutely straight. We found her at her barbecue. She turned at us and waved a gun at us and then just when we was ducking for cover, she stuck it in her mouth and we heard a click. I may not look like much now, but I was a marine. I got to her and took the gun off her and Andy and me brought her back here and I called an ambulance 'cause she was bleeding from her mouth and looked woozy as hell. So you got no call to talk about anything else."

"She hasn't said anything yet," Powder said.

"All right, then," Voss said, nodding around the room. "I may not be no family man now, but that don't make me no pervert."

Powder leaned on the bar and said, "I'll tell you what's bothering me."

"What?"

"The clothes are pretty well burned, even the shoes."

"So?"

"So, I'm bothered because there is nothing to show how she got the fire going."

"That's all right. I can help there."

"How's that?"

"There was a lighter."

Powder eyed the man.

"Andy saw it."

Powder didn't speak.

"Hell, if we didn't pick it up, kids woulda got it from the alley this morning."

Still Powder said nothing.

"Hell, who could think something like that would be important? You want it? I got it here. Look." Voss bent behind the bar to a shelf beneath the cash register. He brought up a small disposable lighter and put it on the bar in front of Powder. "It's just a cruddy lighter. Dime a dozen. But I smoke and Andy doesn't, so I kept it. So what? Hey? So what?"

Powder remained silent.

"What, you lost your tongue all of a sudden? Hey, look, so maybe we touched her up a little bit on the way in. Maybe a little, 'cause she was fogged out and didn't know the difference. And how are you not going to when you're moving somebody in her condition, hey? But nothing else. I swear. Nothing else."

At three-thirty Powder pulled up on Vermont Street in front of the house in which he lived. He occupied the lowest of the three floors, and had five rooms.

The building was a nineteenth-century Italianate

structure that would have looked like an expatriate's long-
ing for home writ large in almost any other part of Indianapolis. But the house was on the edge of the district
centered around and named for Lockerbie Square, and the
variety of imaginative houses built by the wealthy of
nearly a century ago made the area unique in the city.

When flowers were in power Lockerbie was a hippie
haven, but now the spacious houses were fought over by
the new urbanites, who liked the fancifulness of the area
and the fact that it was only ten minutes' walk from Mon-
ument Circle even if they always drove.

Anchored amidst the transient fashionabilities, an old
guard dotted the district, determined to ride out the fuss.
The Civil War had come and gone, and so would trendy
appreciation of these venerable houses that were, after all,
just their homes. The comfortably heeled Hoosier is un-
surpassed in his cranky defense of the status quo.

Powder enjoyed the cultural conflict of his neighborhood immensely, and was a fringe participant in occasional
civic projects. He also did a little manual volunteer work
for the older members of the residents' association and
gave a little law-related advice to the others.

He did not like the fact that his downstairs curtains
were closed.

In the morning he had left them open.

He thought about it for a moment. He got out of his
car. From the tool kit in his trunk, he took a can of pene-
trating oil.

Then he walked to the back of the house and mounted
the wooden stairs to his back porch. There he oiled the
hinges of his kitchen screen door. And he waited two minutes, by his watch.

Carefully, Powder entered the house.

He could hear immediately that there were people inside.

He drew his gun.

He walked to the door of the hallway. Some creaking came from his front room. He thought he heard a whisper.

He waited again, listening for more sounds, suggestions of human activity in other parts of the apartment.

All he heard were inhuman sounds, a house in stasis: refrigerator, clock.

He walked slowly along the hall to the front room.

He settled both hands around the handle of his weapon, took a breath, and kicked the door. It flew open. He jumped in, landed in a crouch, and said, "Police! Don't move!"

The gun pointed up the wrong end of a large, hairy bottom that was connected, in turn, to four bare legs. The legs sprawled and writhed in the middle of the floor. Someone grunted.

The woman said, "Jesus, Ricky, cut it out! Someone's there!"

"What? What?" The hairy bottom's questions were breathless.

As Powder lowered his gun, the man rolled off and sighed. Then he sat up, acknowledging Powder for the first time.

"Hi, Dad," he said. "I didn't expect you home so early."

6

"**S**o, I'm kind of between abodes," Ricky said. "That's an emergency, isn't it? That's what you gave me a key for. And I'd like to crash here for a while. Till I get resettled, you know?"

"You still have your job?"

"Of course I do."

"Why aren't you at work?" Powder asked.

Ricky smiled wryly. "I am," he said. He winked. "What Ma Bell doesn't know can't hurt her."

Powder said nothing.

"The truck is out back. Look, is it all right if I stay here or not?"

Powder shrugged and nodded.

"Great. Thanks, Dad. I'll try to keep out of your way."

"How about cleaning the spots on my rug?"

"Sure, sure. What does it take?" Ricky turned to his woman friend. "You know, Tammy?"

Tammy shook her head. Then said, "Soap and water, I suppose."

"They're little spots, Dad. They'll dry away."

Powder said nothing. He rose from the kitchen chair.

"You'll see," Ricky said.

"I suppose I will," Powder said. He walked out the back door.

The top of an Indiana Bell lineman's truck was clearly visible in the alley, now that he looked for it. Powder stooped to pick up the can of oil and went through the backyard to his garage.

Inside, he examined the front of a bureau drawer. He had intended to add a coat of polyurethane, but instead he trimmed some overflow glue with a linoleum knife and ran his fingers over the dry surface of the last coat. He dabbed at some air bubble irregularities with fine sandpaper, and then put the drawer down and made his way back to his car.

It was twenty past four when he arrived at the office. A stocky man in his early thirties sat behind the counter talking to Sergeant Fleetwood.

"A missing person you're waiting for someone to claim, Sergeant?" Powder asked sharply as he came in.

Fleetwood straightened noticeably in her chair.

"At ease," Powder said before she spoke. "Busy afternoon?"

"I don't know what the norm is, but I don't think it's been particularly busy."

"Pity," Powder said. He took the logbook and began to read it. "I hoped you'd be rushed off your feet." Without looking up, he asked, "Who's your friend?"

"This is Carl Bywater. Lieutenant Powder. Carl made my wheelchair for me."

"That's right," Bywater said. "Sure did."

Powder looked at the man, whose shaggy straw-colored hair swung like a mop as he rose and turned to extend a hand. "Glad to meet you, Lieutenant Powder. Carollee here has been telling me all about you."

Powder returned to his scrutiny of the log entries, which were clearly and precisely written. As Bywater stood, Powder said, "What do you do for a living, Carl? Are you a full-time wheelchair craftsman?"

"Yes sir, I sure am."

Powder's eyebrows rose briefly.

"My uncle Berl runs the sales and rentals side and I do the repairs and the custom work."

"Racing stripes, eh?"

"Well, sir, it's mostly fulfilling an individual's practical requirements and seeing how far we can extend the wheelchair frontier."

Powder straightened and looked at the young man. "And I expect you stopped to see the raven-haired police beauty on her first day on the job to see if there were any bugs in the chair."

"Uh, that's right. Yes, sir. Sure did."

"And are there any bugs?"

"Uh, no. Not really."

"No bugs at all. Well, that's mighty fine work, Mr. Bywater. I expect Carollee's real grateful. And it's a tribute to the quality control on your production line. Congratulations."

"Uh, thank you."

"I'd like to shake your hand on that fine piece of work."

Powder shook the man's hand.

"Hope to see you again sometime soon, Mr. Bywater."

"Uh, right. Guess I'll be running along now." He raised the counter flap and passed through the gap.

"Keep up the good work," Powder said.

"Uh, yes, sir. Sure will. Bye now. Bye, Carollee."

"Good-bye, Carl."

Powder waited until the office door closed. He turned to Fleetwood. "Try to keep your swain's attentions con-

fined to out-of-hours, will you, Sergeant? And keep civil-
ians on the other side of the counter."

"He was looking at the chair," she said.

"I don't care if he was adjusting your truss."

"In any event, you don't have to—"

"I've got an errand for you," Powder said, interrupt-
ing. "I want you to run up to Forensic and give them this
lighter. Tell them it goes with the burned clothes I left earlier and I want to know if there's anything about it that
might help an identification. A long shot, but we do our
best. Got it?"

The log showed that his new sergeant had dealt with
six people. Three log entries had come to the office and
three had telephoned. The office visitors had all been potential new cases, two adult and one juvenile.

Although people of all ages who were reported as
missing went onto the Reportable Incident file, only juvenile cases were pursued as a matter of routine. And for the
bulk of these, older teen-agers, the searches were generally
uneventful, done from a checklist: initial phone calls and
visits, and then follow-up calls at administratively established intervals as long as the case was open. More often
than not the juveniles were located, even if that was no
guarantee of their return to the fold from which they had
absented themselves. Missing sub-fourteen-year-olds auto-
matically went to Detectives.

People missing adults often contacted the office, but
most did not bother to complete the "long form" when
they realized that Powder and his staff would take no active steps to find the missing party. For the most part,
leaving home or work, as such, was not against the law.
Crimes were generally referred to other departments,
which left Powder to work primarily on cases that had features of extra interest, or that he felt like working on.

The refinements of these judgments were hard to convey, first day, to a new sergeant. Fleetwood had handled her contacts strictly by the book.

Her best work was with a woman concerned about a daughter absent over the weekend. Fleetwood had taken her through the procedure, and had found that not all the possible places the girl might be had yet been eliminated. The woman had been sent to the public telephones in the hall around the corner and had found her daughter. A saving of several taxpayer dimes.

The two other callers in the office were men missing women. One had left after hearing that the department would not punish his wife if they did find her. He'd said he had a pretty damn good idea where she was.

The second man, missing a girlfriend, had begun the form and then gone home to get supplementary material to complete it with.

Fleetwood had also dealt with three telephone calls.

Major Tafelski had made his Monday inquiry about "the search" for his missing sister. She had been gone for nearly seven years.

A man had asked how one went about listing a wife as a missing person.

And the last call had been to report that a seventeen-year-old son had returned home.

Powder closed the log, happy enough that Fleetwood had had a varied if not frantic dip in the Missing Persons pool. It seemed she would swim.

He went to the manual Male file, where the case forms relating to Indianapolis's missing men were stored in order of birth date.

There he spent ten minutes leafing through photographs of men who had been born between 1915 and 1945. He compared them with the photograph of the unidentified male corpse he had taken at County Hospital in the morning.

He pulled three cases, but without confidence. The corpse had a couple of weeks' growth of beard, which masked some features. But Powder's guess was that it wasn't on record.

Then he turned to preparing for Fleetwood a list of the thirty-, sixty-, and hundred-and-twenty-day follow-up phone calls that were due in the week. The department had a card file, rather like those of precomputer libraries, in which case calls moved to the front of the racks as they came due.

Two men walked in.

Man day, Powder thought. Manday Monday.

The younger was dressed in a tattered gray jacket and baggy trousers. He was unshaved and he carried a small plastic bag, which he lifted carefully to the counter space.

The second man held back. Perhaps forty, he wore a well-blocked navy-blue sweater with the collar of the underlying shirt turned out over the crew neck. He seemed a trim, well-organized figure and Powder spoke to him first.

"If you would care to sit in one of the chairs, I'll be with you as soon as I've seen to this gentleman."

The older man pivoted to look for the chairs.

The younger man said, "I talked to someone else when I came before. She sent me home to get some stuff." He fingered the plastic bag.

"Ah," Powder said. "You would be Mr. Burrus."

"Yeah. Right." He took a pack of cigarettes from his inside jacket pocket.

"This is a no-smoking zone," Powder said.

"Oh. Hell. Sorry," Burrus said. He put the cigarettes away. "I went back to my place to look for a few things." He began to empty the plastic bag. "Like I told the lady, I don't have a picture. That's the way she was. Is. She'd be there sometimes and then not." The man shrugged, seeking sympathy. "After nearly a year. I know her birthday, but not how old she is. Her taste in music—none. And some pictures she drew. And I've got some clothing sizes, and a few other things." He picked them out and named them one by one.

Powder watched and listened as the recital ran its course. He thought of a magician, pulling things from a hat. Ta dah! And didn't notice at first when Burrus had finished.

Powder said, "As my colleague spoke to you earlier, I think it would be best if you were to speak to her again."

"Yeah? Well, OK. Where do I go?"

"You stay here. I'll track her down for you."

Powder called Forensic on the internal telephone. "Is Sergeant Fleetwood there?"

They knew immediately that she was. Everybody knew Fleetwood. She came to the telephone. "Lieutenant Powder? I was waiting here because they said they were about to have preliminary information on the items you gave them this morning."

"There is a Mr. Burrus down here. He has brought in a kitchen sink and other artifacts from his ruined life. As you know what you asked for and why, I thought you might care to stop being flirted with and come down and do some work."

Powder hung up. "She'll be with you in a couple of minutes," he said.

As Burrus fidgeted, Powder moved along the counter and hailed the man sitting across the room.

"What can we do for you?" Powder asked as he came to the desk.

"I phoned an hour and a half ago. I want to report that my wife is missing."

"Yes sir. Your name?"

"William G. Weaver, Junior."

"And your wife's name?"

"Annie. Not Ann. Maiden name, Coates. No middle name."

"I see. Address?"

"Thirty-seven Twenty-eight Oxford Street."

"And your wife's date of birth?"

"January twenty-sixth, 1952."

"Where was she born?"

"Quincy, Illinois."

"All right," Powder said, looking up. "Tell me about it."

"It? Oh, the circumstances."

"That's right."

"She wasn't home on Saturday when I got back from the store. It is really just about that simple."

"What kind of store is that, Mr. Weaver?"

"I run a small security-hardware business. Locks, alarms, that kind of thing."

"Where is this?"

"On Massachusetts Avenue, just northeast of the junction with Tenth Street. It's called Lock and Key."

"I take it that your wife is ordinarily at home when you get back from the store on a Saturday."

"Invariably. I would say that there have been no exceptions for ten years."

"Until two days ago."

"That's right."

"What do you think has happened, Mr. Weaver?"

"I think she's run away. Her clothes are gone, cleared out. And she took a substantial amount of money out of the bank on Friday afternoon."

"I see," Powder said, making notes.

Behind him Fleetwood opened the back door and,

bumping the frame twice, made her way into the office.

Powder took William Weaver to the separated counter area and continued his questions.

"You were saying that your wife ... that Annie took money out of the bank on Friday afternoon."

"Yes."

"When did you learn about this?"

"This morning."

"How?"

"I asked the bank."

"You suspected she might have taken money?"

"She was gone. She would need money."

"A joint account?"

"Yes."

"How much did she take?"

"Seven hundred and fifty dollars."

"How much is left in the account?"

"Two hundred and thirty-eight."

"Why didn't she take that?"

"I don't know."

"What was she unhappy about?"

"Excuse me?"

"What was she unhappy about? Why did she leave?"

Expressionlessly, Weaver said, "I don't know."

"You don't know. She didn't leave a note?"

"A suicide wouldn't pack clothes and take money."

Powder frowned and scolded the man. "You don't have to have your hand on a bottle of pills to write a note. Did she leave you anything at all giving you some idea where or why she went, or how long she would be gone for?"

"Nothing," Weaver said.

"What special or unusual happened recently?"

"Nothing at all. We lived a very settled, regular life."

"Any children?"

"No."

"Does your wife have any close friends?"

Weaver hesitated. "Not really."

"What does that mean?"

"She has a few people she goes out with. Women. I don't know how close they are."

"And she was at home every day, or just Saturdays?"

"She worked in the store three days a week—Monday, Wednesday, and Friday. Unless I was away on a business trip."

"How often do you go away on a business trip?"

"Now, perhaps every month or so. Generally for the weekend, but sometimes for a couple of days during the week."

"Was there anything that your wife might have found out about these trips which could have upset her?"

"Nothing whatsoever."

"And while you were away, she was in the store full-time?"

"Yes."

"How did she spend her time on the other days?"

"Primarily in housekeeping."

"And you have no idea why she should go away?"

"None at all."

"How long have you been married, Mr. Weaver?"

"Since May thirtieth, 1971."

"And have there been any little hiccups or big hiccups in that time?"

"No."

"No problems? Neither of you left home for a time?"

"No."

"Neither of you sought consolation elsewhere for some reason or another or for no reason at all?"

"You mean affairs?"

"That sort of thing."

"No. I mean, I can't speak for my wife—"

"Annie."

"Yes. I can't speak for her with the same authority I can for myself, but no, not as far as I know."

"She is a good deal younger than yourself."

"Yes."

"You've sensed no restlessness in her?"

"None at all."

"And there has been nothing unusual that happened recently."

"No."

"What about in the near future? Did you expect anything unusual to be happening soon?"

"No." Weaver hesitated. "Well . . ."

"What?"

"We were planning to go camping at the end of this week. We had never done that before."

"Was Annie looking forward to that?"

"Yes," Weaver said, but his tone conveyed doubt.

"You're not sure?"

"It was my idea. That we do something a bit different. She said she was happy to give it a try."

"You're not suggesting that she ran out on your marriage to keep from going camping?"

"No," Weaver said stiffly. "But you asked about things out of the ordinary."

"So," Powder said, "she's never left home before?"

"Never."

"I suppose you have checked with her parents and other relatives?"

"Her parents are dead. I checked with everyone else I could think of."

"Mr. Weaver, do you suspect foul play?"

"Foul play? You mean—"

"Murder. Kidnap."

"Well," he said, "no."

"Nothing really to indicate it, eh?"

"That's right. Nothing."

"In fact, all that is indicated is that she left home because she felt like a change."

"She is not impulsive. She likes things just so."

"Like yourself."

"Yes."

"Yet you can't suggest anything else."

"No."

"Mr. Weaver, I would like to ask you another question."

"What is that?"

"Why are you here?"

"Here?"

"In the Missing Persons office of the Indianapolis Police Department. What exactly is it that you expect us to do for you here?"

"I'm not certain what you can do."

"All right. Why did you come here?"

"To report my wife as missing."

"As a fact? Like registering a birth or a death?"

"It is a fact. Is it not something that one is obliged to do?"

"Is there something about your wife's disappearance you thought we should be interested in, from the police side of things?"

"I felt it should be on record."

"I see."

"She is missing," he said.

Powder asked, "Do you miss her?"

"Well, she's not there."

Powder leaned back and looked at the man's expressionless face. Then he bent to draw a long form from beneath counter level. "OK," he said. "I am going to want a photograph, all the personal records she left behind, like checkbook, address book, letters. And if you have anything which is likely to have her fingerprints on it, I am going to want that too."

"I brought a photograph with me," Weaver said.

It was five-thirty when William Weaver left the office. Powder locked the door behind him and turned to Fleetwood, who was at her desk.

He passed through the counter gap and approached her from behind. Suddenly genial, Powder said, "Your first day in Missing Persons. Was it as much fun as you expected it to be?"

She backed her chair away from the desk and faced him. He saw how utterly exhausted she was. She said, "Lovely."

Powder turned hard. "What do you make of your Mr. Burrus?"

"His girlfriend has cut out," Fleetwood said slowly. She tossed the hair from her cheek. "He can't conceive why she would do that."

"Why would she?"

"From what he says, she is unpredictable at the best of times."

"Spell it out for me, Sergeant."

"He's known her for less than a year and until three months ago she wouldn't stay over with him even on occasional nights. Then one day she moved in, though she kept her own place. No explanation why she decided to stay. She isn't much of an explainer and from what I gather he was afraid to ask too many questions. She's moody and what he calls high-strung."

"What is his stringing?"

"He seems a natural plodder who tries hard to pretend he's instinctive."

Powder said, "That a big strong on the judgment and perception, isn't it?"

Fleetwood shrugged.

"If you're so strong on your own instincts, then tell me why the girlfriend left."

"Who knows?"

"Make me a guess, Sergeant."

"OK," Fleetwood said. "I say she's left because he was trying to lock her into the housewife bit."

"So what's happened to her?"

"She's lying in a bathtub somewhere, holding her crotch, and breathing sighs of relief like a machine gun."

Powder rubbed his face. Then he said, "I got one who doesn't know why the wife left him too."

"That accountant type?"

"You seem a little hard on quiet men," Powder said.

Fleetwood said nothing.

"I'd like you to have a look at the file I've opened on him." He dropped the folder on the desk beside her.

"Any special reason?"

"It'll give us something to talk about tomorrow morning."

Fleetwood looked at the file. "I've got an hour of physio now."

Powder asked slowly, "Are you on those sticks at all yet?"

"Sure."

"Physio after work," Powder said. "So the therapist is a friend, maybe. And stretches the point on progress reports, maybe." Powder shook his head and cleared his throat. "Dynamite, kid. That's really terrific."

Fleetwood said nothing.

7

*P*owder went up to the Forensic Lab.

It was closed.

In the detective dayroom, he had a pigeonhole, and when he went and looked in it he found the preliminary forensic report. Also, separately, the fingerprint inquiry result on his unidentified male.

The unidentified male was not on file with the IPD. Powder overwrote on the memo that the prints should be checked with the FBI and put the notice into another pigeonhole.

The forensic report showed that the would-be amnesiac's partially burned clothes had mixed potential for providing identification information.

The underwear was chain bought and "not the cheapest."

Skirt and blouse were homemade, from heavy, high-quality cloth. The sewing had been done by hand, and the garments were well worn.

Summer sandals were cheap and light, probably bought recently.

And there was a belt, an elasticized-cloth souvenir type designed in blue and white with a name repeated over its length. The name was Aurora.

* * *

Powder arrived at County Hospital at mealtime. He found his Jane Doe faced with a bed tray bearing two large glasses, each of which had a straw. Her mouth seemed less puffy than it had in the morning, but the face more gray, as if the darkness around the eyes were spreading.

"Hello, Aurora," Powder said cheerfully.

The woman coughed.

"Had a good day? Hey, don't let me interrupt your meal, Aurora. You've got to eat to get healthy and big and strong again. Right, Aurora?"

She frowned at him and exercised her jaw a few times before saying, "Why do you call me that?" Her voice was still blurry.

"It's your name, isn't it?"

She was silent in the face of this question, but Powder gave her little chance to seem not to remember.

He sat down heavily in the chair by her bed. "Dear, dear. I've had a long day, Aurora. Quite a strain."

He rubbed his face.

"Hey, what do you know, Aurora? I've got a new sergeant in my department who can't walk. But she's told the higher-ups that she can. What do you think of that? The book says that I ought to go to the brass and sort it out. I've been a book cop all my life, but problem is, the bastards'll replace her with a dummy. What do you think?"

The woman stared.

"See, there are maybe twenty-five guys in the force already who are too fat to run faster than this gal can wheel herself, so who am I to say that in a department the size of the one in Indianapolis there is no place for one officer in a wheelchair? Is that for me to decide? What would you say? Nothing? You think I should do nothing? Probably good advice. Except it may put me at risk, just when I am trying to build my section's importance up. Does that matter, you think?"

Nothing.

"On the other hand," Powder said easily as he shifted position in the chair, "I find I don't have quite the same drive to sort the world out that I used to. Maybe I'm getting old, eh? I do know that I sit and wonder at the energy of my part-time secretary. Girl called Agnes Shorter. You know her? No, of course you wouldn't. But she gets through more secretarial work than I can dream up for her and then has time to develop the computer side of the job too. She doesn't seem to have any other interests, but that's not my problem. Hey, don't let me put you off your food. Drink up. Couple of teeth out makes good room for the straws, eh?"

Powder stopped talking for a moment. He leaned forward and pushed the tray a little closer to the woman. She took one of the glasses and began to drink.

"Hungry, huh? Good sign. And you know," Powder said, "on top of all that, I've got troubles with my son. I'm divorced, see, and ever since the breakup, my time with the kid has been real strained. Sides with his mother, though he's shifty enough I wouldn't be surprised if he sides with me when he's with her. Thinks the world owes him a living, as far as I can tell. Not that he's sponging off us. Kid's got a job, but miles below his potential. What he hasn't got is a sense of responsibility, you know. *Responsibility,* you know what I mean?

The woman remained silent.

"Do you know what I mean, Aurora?"

She said nothing.

"Aurora, you're not pulling your weight here. I'm doing all the talking and when I ask you a civil question, even then you don't say anything. I'm beginning to think that you're not interested in my problems or in why I've had such a tiring day."

Nothing.

"Silent treatment, eh? Well, let me tell you about one more problem I've got, Aurora. Aurora. Hard name to make a nickname from, eh? But on top of all these other problems and on top of my basic job itself—which is heart-breaking stuff, kids leaving home, telling their parents they can't stand them anymore, running out. Even sometimes murder and kidnap. And the adults, leaving home and hurting just as much as kids, only we don't have time to work on finding them. On top of all that, I've also got a goddamn self-indulgent woman in the hospital playing dumb-ass games about not knowing who she is and wasting my time and everybody's money that could be spent on better things. What do you think about that?"

The woman did not respond.

"Agree with me that it shows no sense of responsibility, do you?"

The woman shifted her position in the bed for the first time.

Powder exhaled heavily, and leaned forward. In a slower, more formal voice he said, "I told you this morning that I don't believe you have amnesia."

"I don't remember anything," she said suddenly, as if slapping his face.

"You stuck a gun in your mouth and pulled the trigger. To me that means you know only too well who you are."

"Who I am is nobody's business."

Powder spread his hands to encompass the whole of the problem. "But it *is*, Aurora," he said. "In the whole of the goddamn, unjust, and cruel world, I am the one person whose business it literally is."

Her eyes dropped to her drinks.

"I don't mean to minimize such anguish as inclined you to chew on a gun barrel, but you give me no chance to help or even sympathize. And I am not just going to go away. Put yourself in my boots. Hypothetical situation. What do you do if you are me and you as you continue to play hard to identify?"

"I don't know. What do I do?"

"You take your fingerprints and add them to the stuff the ID people are already working on, which includes your burned clothes. Then in a day or two your picture gets spread all over the newspapers and TV. And then impressions of the teeth you've got left get sent to all the dentists. And it doesn't rest, my dear Aurora, until you have been identified. Because, believe me, I will identify you, Aurora."

The woman was distinctly uneasy.

"So the question is, what is the point of all this work and time and trouble? I'd be a lot happier putting in the same time and effort trying to sort out your difficulties. Maybe I can help and maybe not. But no way does it make sense for you to do anything but tell me who you are."

Powder spread his hands again, and put an expression on his face that he felt, inside, to be an irresistibly supportive and trustworthy one. Faced with the expression he felt was on his face, he would confide his middle name.

The woman looked at him and thought. But did not speak. Then she turned away to bury her face in her pillow.

The tray across her body bounced. The two glasses tipped over.

Powder sat and watched for a moment. In a wave he felt the great tiredness, the great pointlessness that he had claimed for himself at the beginning of the confrontation.

He rose and left.

* * *

In the corridor he met the slightly built nurse with the large eyes and commanding manner he had spoken to on his way out in the morning.

"How's your bedside manner this evening?" she asked him.

"In truly peak form."

"Have you got her name yet?"

"Yeah. Jane Doe. Look, how strong is she? Physically."

"She's all right. Why?"

"I've upset her and threatened her."

"You're saying she might skip out in the night?"

"I guess so."

"You better put someone on her door."

"If I did that, I'd have to book her. I'd rather pass that until I know it's the right way to go."

"All I can do is make it hard for her to get access to outdoor clothes and tell my nurses to keep an eye out."

Powder nodded slowly.

"Thanks," he said, eventually. Then, "How come you don't look as tired as I feel?"

"Because I love my job."

"I just wondered," Powder said. He walked to the elevator.

8

Powder stopped at Johnson's, a neighborhood grocery store, on his way home. Open till ten every night, it was run by a family of many members whose several destinies were controlled by a man who seemed to be the uncle of all the others. They called him Uncle Adg and his given name, Agile, was as ironic as it was unusual considering that he was singularly fat. Powder had never seen him stir from the store's stock room. But however god-uncly Adg's absolutism in the family, his dealings with Powder about neighborhood issues were always temperate and polite.

As Powder stood before a frozen-food cabinet, one of the nieces noticed him and stopped restocking shelves nearby.

"Evening, Mr. Powder."

"Evening. Janice, isn't it?"

"That's right. You got a minute, Mr. Powder?"

"I guess so."

"I know Uncle Adg would like to see you, if you got a minute."

Powder nodded. "I was getting a headache trying to choose here anyway."

He followed Janice to the stock room, where Adg was working on a clipboard.

"Mr. Powder. Thank you for sparing a moment."

"That's OK. What can I do for you?"

"John Parrun, of the residents' association, you know him?"

"Sure."

"He was talking today about something he sees as a danger to us all."

"What would that be?" Powder asked quietly.

"These." Johnson held out a leaflet. Powder took it and read about a special offer on insulation inspection.

"I don't understand."

"They are being put in people's mailboxes. And you see? There's no address on it."

"Yes?"

"I called the number on the bottom. It's just a funny sound. Like, maybe, disconnected."

Powder waited.

"We think it may be a dodge."

"How?"

"It's June. Getting into prime vacation time. If leaflets are put into mailboxes so a corner can be seen from the road, then you can tell which houses are empty from people going away."

Powder rubbed his face. "What an untrusting fellow you are, Mr. Johnson."

"You can do all the right things, going on vacation. Stop the papers, leave a light on, have the mail held. Someone comes along and puts this in the box and everybody knows that you're away."

"OK," Powder said. "I'll have it looked into."

"Thanks. Everyone will be grateful."

Powder went back to the frozen-food cabinet. He read the leaflet.

Janice Johnson, still at work on shelves, asked, "Can I help you, Mr. Powder?"

"Yeah," Powder said forcefully. "Yeah."

"How?"

"Tell me what kids eat these days."

As Powder entered his apartment's front door, Ricky appeared in the hallway almost immediately. He came from the living room and pulled the door closed behind him. Two wires trailed through the hall to Powder's spare bedroom.

"Hey, Dad. How you doing?"

"Great," Powder said. He walked to the kitchen and began unpacking his shopping bag.

Ricky followed. He said, "I've got a few friends in. We're going out for a big feed in a few minutes. One of them is late. And I wanted to hang around till you got back so I could let you know not to worry."

"I won't worry."

"And I'll try not to disturb you when I come in, or anything like that."

"OK."

"And thanks again for letting me stay at such short notice. I'll be out looking for a permanent place tomorrow."

Powder turned from the refrigerator and asked, "Day off?"

"No, no. But you know what I mean. I'll keep an eye out, put the word around, that kind of thing."

"I know what you mean," Powder said.

"OK," Ricky said. "That's fine."

"I think I'll come in and meet your friends," Powder said.

"What?"

Powder left the kitchen and walked to the living room. Ricky scuttled after him.

"The wires are for my speakers," Ricky said edgily. "I

put some music on and didn't want to impose by using your hi-fi."

"Thanks," Powder said. "They got their clothes on in there?" He walked into the living room ahead of his son. "Stand by your beds," he said.

Darting in behind, Ricky said, "Smokes out, people. I'd like to introduce my father."

Two men and two women, all in their early twenties, sat in the room. Three stubbed cigarettes out in coffee cups.

"I warned them, see," Ricky said. "You don't like smoking."

The aroma in the room was of uncomplicatedly commercial origin. "What a waste of good tobacco," Powder said. "I'm Roy Powder, Ricky's dad." He stood in front of the nearest visitor. "Who are you?"

Startled, the man rose. "John Hurst," he said.

"I'm a detective lieutenant in the police department, John Hurst. What do you do?"

"Uh, I work for the post office."

"Pleased to make your acquaintance," Powder said. He shook Hurst's hand.

"I also work for a community newspaper. As an investigative reporter."

"Must be fascinating," Powder said. He moved to the woman next to Hurst.

"I'm Rebecca Coffey," she said.

Powder shook hands with her. "Do you work?" he asked.

"Not for money."

"And probably all the harder for that."

A pudgy man with blond curls rose as Powder passed to face him. "Dwayne Grove," he said. "I work for the phone company, like Ricky."

"A colleague from work," Powder said. "How folksy."

"Only I've got the easy end of the job. Indoors, with accounts and records."

"I see," Powder said.

Turning to the second woman he asked, "And you?"

"Lila Lee. I work for the Department of the Interior, in the geological survey department."

"Glad to meet you, Ms. Lee."

"It's Mrs. Lee," she said.

"Apologies," Powder said.

"My husband is away."

Expansively, Powder said, "Pleased to meet you all. Any friends of Ricky's are friends of mine. His *casa* is your *casa*." Powder dropped to the floor in a cross-legged position and picked up one of the cups. "There's more than half of this cigarette left," he said. "Is this one yours, Mrs. Lee? I don't know much about them, but is it relightable?"

"Uh, no."

"Well, have another. Go on. Have a fresh one."

Lila Lee found a pack of cigarettes in her purse. Taking one she offered the pack around.

Powder was saying, "I don't think cigarettes are nearly the worst thing for public health there is around these days." He smiled sweetly at Rebecca, a sallow woman with a lean face and very small ears.

"Oh?" she said vacantly.

Ricky was clearly ill at ease, but Dwayne Grove asked, "What do you consider worse than cigarettes, Lieutenant?"

"Oh, don't call me 'Lieutenant' here, Dwayne Grove," Powder said. " 'Sir' will do just fine." He looked sternly around the room, then broke into a loud, short laugh. "What's worse than smoking? I'll tell you. Eating is worse than smoking."

"Eating?" Grove asked. Everyone but Ricky smiled.

"No joke," Powder said. "No joke."

"What, you mean additives and all the stuff like that?" Lila Lee asked.

"No," Powder said. "I mean food, generally and specifically."

"I don't understand," she said.

"It is simple enough, Mrs. Lee. You are, perhaps, five feet six inches in height and of so-called normal weight."

"I hope so," she said.

"Normal, by the charts for weight and height that are on all the public scales."

"Yes."

"If you weighed less," Powder said, "six or seven percent less, then your life expectancy, already high, would be extended by several months. Do you catch my drift?"

"I guess so."

"My drift is that 'underweight' people live longer than 'normal'-weight people, Mrs. Lee."

"Yes?"

"Yes, indeed," Powder said. "So if that is the case then it is indisputable that in any amount greater than that required to keep you 'underweight,' food kills."

"But almost everybody weighs more than those charts."

"Therefore food is a pervasive social evil, and consumption of food should be actively discouraged by society," Powder said.

"I like it. I like it," John Hurst said. "Health warnings on everything you eat."

"Definitely. Banning of food advertising. Punitive taxation on high-calorie food."

"Another antisocial ploy of the big corporations, trying to make us all eat more and more and more," Hurst said, nodding. "Think of the food commercials on TV. They're killing us all for profit. I never really thought about it before."

Powder rose abruptly. "But hey, my boy here says that you are all going out for a big meal, right?"

Hurst nodded.

"A bit of a celebration, eh?"

Looking at the others before speaking, Lila Lee said, "I think you could call it that."

"Gee," Powder said. "All this talk about food ... I wouldn't put you off your feed for the world."

9

*T*o Powder's surprise, Ricky joined him at breakfast.

"Hey, my people really liked you," Ricky said.

Powder was silent.

"Really. There's a party Friday night and they want you to come."

"Groovy," Powder said.

"No, Dad. Things aren't groovy much anymore."

"Your people," Powder said. "Do they live near here?"

"Yeah, they all live within striking distance. I don't know how you managed to get a place in this part of town on your salary, but this is definitely the place to be in Indianapolis. Apartments in this area just can't be had these days."

"You were up near your mother's, weren't you?"

"The old house, yeah, right."

"How is your mother?"

"I haven't seen her for a few weeks."

"But you were living up there."

"Well, not just lately. I moved into Speedway, but then that didn't work out. There's nothing and nobody out in Speedway."

"Except Tammy?"

Ricky smiled. "She's not important to me," he said earnestly. "More and more my important friends—business and pleasure—live around here."

"What kind of business would that be?"

"Never wise to have all the eggs in one basket," Ricky said lightly.

"Chicken farming, are you?"

Ricky exaggerated a mysterious smile.

"How *was* your mother, then?"

"OK. Fine."

"Great?"

"Yeah, great."

"Superb?"

"Yeah, pretty superb." Ricky hesitated. "What do you mean?"

"So, where does this party Friday take place?"

"You know Rebecca, from last night?"

"Yes."

"Well she has a house, actually on Lockerbie Street. It's real old, like maybe pre-1900, and it has these churchy-type windows."

"She owns it?"

"Her husband and her."

"Which one was her husband?"

Ricky looked away momentarily. "Her husband wasn't there."

"I see."

"But there's one thing. It's not really a problem, but it's something you should know."

"And what would that be?"

"It's a costume party."

Powder was silent.

"You know. Costumes. Not that you would have to, or even be expected to, but you should know."

"I see."

"They really want you to come. They were very impressed."

"Did you have a good meal last night?"

"Really good. I took them to the Gin Tub. It's up north on—"

"I know where it is. You took them?"

"Yeah, well. It was kind of a return for a favor or two. Dwayne put me onto some private wiring work and I did a little job for Lila, so this was by way of thanks."

"Dwayne. The one in telephone records?"

Puzzling, Ricky said, "Yeah." Then, "But you should go to the Gin Tub sometime. The food was special. None of this 'natural'-food crap that breaks off pieces of your teeth. All really prepared and cooked stuff."

Powder stood up. "What do you want for breakfast?"

"Is there some cereal?"

"I just happened to get some in yesterday," Powder said. "It's new. Uncooked grains of rice, house dust, dried oak leaves, and very small pieces of carpet, for natural fiber."

"What?" Ricky didn't understand. "Any Sugar Puffs?"

"Damn. Ran out yesterday."

"I think I'll just have a cup of coffee," Ricky said.

"Coffee," Powder said. "Groovy."

The day was gray and wet.

Before he went to his car, Powder stopped at the two-floor brick house next door to the west. The house had a cast-iron balcony that overhung the front door and dripped rusty water in the light rain. He rang the bell and stood in front of the door for a long time. Finally it opened and a broad, stooped woman peered out.

"Mrs. Cook, I stopped to tell you that your drawer will take another day."

"Oh?"

"I said I would have it for you today, but it won't be finished until tomorrow."

"That's the way with everything anymore. Nothing happens when it's supposed to."

"Not till tomorrow morning."

"Tomorrow morning. Oh. Oh, that's all right. Thank you very much, Mr. Powder."

"That's quite all right."

"Mr. Powder?"

"Yes?"

"Yesterday. Yesterday I saw a young couple at your door. In the afternoon. They stood there and then they went in. I wondered whether I should do something about it, but then I saw you out front."

"The young man is my son, Mrs. Cook, and he had a key."

"Oh. How nice."

"He's going to be staying with me for a while."

"You're a very lucky man, Mr. Powder."

"I'll have the drawer for you tomorrow."

10

When he saw the head nurse, Powder could tell that something was wrong. She was on the telephone but as soon as she recognized him her face darkened to forebode the fierceness of an April thunderstorm.

When it came it missed only the lightning.

"I suppose you already know that we notified your people in the night."

"My people?"

"You're a policeman, aren't you?" she asked rhetorically and with considerable irritation.

"What has happened?" Powder asked.

"Your 'Jane Doe'—" she began archly.

Powder interrupted. "Is she still here?"

"In a manner of speaking."

"What the hell has happened?"

"The hell that has happened is that your 'Jane Doe' was found in the toilets last night. She had scored her face with the edge of a broken bottle."

Powder stared.

"My duty nurse heard the bottle breaking, but it took her a few minutes to locate it. The poor woman's face looked like a piece of raw beef."

Although it was already plenty, Powder could tell that there was more.

"It was a disinfectant bottle. She found a cleaning closet door and she drank everything she could find. Bleach, everything. Then she did the work on her face. My nurse stopped her, and called for help. She was rushed to intensive care, and she is still under close observation."

"I see."

"We *try* not to treat attempted suicides as if they're a lower class of patient here, though it's difficult for a lot of nurses since we see so much pain that is not self-inflicted. But last night you said that you had upset this woman. In my book that makes you responsible and irresponsible. I would be most grateful if you would arrange for someone with a degree of sensitivity to do whatever visiting is necessary in the future. Do I make myself clear?"

Powder arrived at Missing Persons earlier even than usual. He tried to fill the time by dealing with paperwork. But his mind wasn't on it. He ended doodling on a pad, and wondering if anybody remembered droodles.

He drew a face, then scored it, as if it were graph paper.

Out loud he said, "Phooey."

Five minutes before the office opening time, a woman tapped on the Missing Persons door. She was plump and wore a dark shawl and looked agitated.

Powder let her in.

"This Missing Persons?" the woman asked as she walked in.

"That's right."

She followed Powder closely and shifted impatiently from foot to foot as he took his place behind the counter.

"I name Mrs. Woods. It my niece. She not show up last night. I telephone my sister and she put her on bus herself and we wait and wait and she don't show up. I telephone bus and bus get in, but girl, she gone."

Powder explained that he had to take details before he could ask more about what had happened.

"OK, mister," the woman said. "I know. Red tape. Girl name Gilkis. Marianna."

Powder recorded the names and addresses. "All right, Mrs. Woods. How old is your niece?"

"Twenty years of age, being twenty-one in November on seventh."

"And where was she traveling from?"

"She come from St. Paul on Greyhound. Changing over Chicago. Bus head on Cincinnati, but she ticket here."

"Might she have gotten off in Chicago?"

"She know nobody Chicago. She know nobody here, only me, her auntie. She come live here, try to work. She come live permanent, you know? Jake Woods, husband, he dead. I alone."

"How was the girl to get from the bus station to your house?"

"Taxi. Her momma, my sister, she give money for that, tell her how, all simple. No buses to house, gotta change, all that."

Powder nodded thoughtfully. "All right, Mrs. Woods," he said. "I'm going to send you upstairs, to the Detective Division."

"You no cop?"

"Yes, I'm a cop, but I can't easily leave here to go out and find what happened to your niece. The people who can go out are upstairs."

The woman nodded gravely. "All again."

"Yes. Take this form. Give it to them and tell them about it. If there is a problem, come back to me. All right?"

"Problem my niece."

"I mean if you have problems upstairs. You ask whoever you talk to for his name and if there is a problem, you come back down here and I'll look into it."

"All right, mister. What your name?"

Powder took the woman to the information desk inside the main door on Alabama Street. Carollee Fleetwood was behind the Missing Persons counter when Powder returned.

"You weren't early," Powder said. "I like my people to be early."

"Tough," Fleetwood said.

Agnes Shorter entered behind them, and as she passed Powder, he handed her a pile of routine work that he had not managed to think about before opening hours.

To Fleetwood he said, "What did you make of the file I gave you to take home?"

Fleetwood took the folder from the pouch behind her seat. "What do I make of it? It's dull. What am I supposed to make of it?"

"That's it exactly!" Powder said. He pounded a fist on his desk top.

As if on cue, William G. Weaver, Jr., walked into the office.

"Ah, Mr. Weaver. My colleague and I were just talking about you."

"You were?" Weaver said mildly.

"We were just commenting on how well you seem to be taking what must be a very trying and upsetting time for you."

"I suppose it is," he said. "Yes."

"Such a settled pattern for years and then without warning a cornerstone, a very linchpin of your life, suddenly, is gone. You must be suffering great turmoil."

"I am doing my best to cope with the situation."

"And very well too," Powder said. "Congratulations."

"Thank you," Weaver said slowly, slightly puzzled. Then, "I brought in some of the items you asked for." He lifted a small carrying case to counter level and set it before Powder.

"Good. Thank you."

Weaver opened the case and began to take things out.

"There weren't really that many of my wife's things left to gather. She took just about everything. But I do have her birth certificate, our marriage license, her high school diploma, and also her checkbook. I've contacted our dentist and doctor and asked them to give you any assistance you ask for, and I've written their names and addresses on a card for you. Also the details of three friends. And there are a few things which might have her fingerprints on them."

"No charge cards?"

"No. She seems to have taken them."

"Good," Powder said. He turned to Sergeant Fleetwood. "You're ready to go out, then?"

"What?"

"Mr. Weaver, I would like you to show your house and business premises to my colleague, Sergeant Fleetwood. All right?"

"Well," Weaver said hesitantly. He looked at Fleetwood. "If you think it's necessary."

"It's just routine. She will drive her own car and she has your home address. She'll meet you there. We often find that missing wives leave things in strange places, so she'll want to make a thorough examination. Any physical help you can give her maneuvering around would be appreciated."

"All right," Weaver said.

"As I said, just routine." Powder held the counter flap up and, without speaking, Fleetwood passed through the gap and left the office with William Weaver.

11

*P*owder was completing some juvenile-case closures when the internal telephone rang. He answered it, saying, "Missing Persons."

"That Powder?"

"Yeah. Who's that, please?"

"Greenwell. Detective Sergeant."

"What can I do for you, Detective Sergeant Greenwell?"

"You can stop sending people up here who take names if we don't drop everything, including our drawers, to scour the streets for AWOL twenty-year-olds."

Stiffly, Powder said, "There is prima facie evidence of kidnap. And my office is not adequately staffed to follow it up."

"Kidnap? You gotta be joking."

"I'm not joking."

"Is there a ransom demand you haven't told us about or something? Shit! Twenty-year-old girls get lost every day, and damn well celebrate it. So do nineteen-year-olds and eighteen-year-olds."

"What's your first name, Sergeant?"

"Now look, Powder . . ."

"Name!"

"Jack. But look, I heard about you too, Lieutenant. And this is just another of your time-wasting referrals."

"If you haven't got time to do your job up there, then work longer hours, work faster, or work better."

"Just what the hell do you expect me to do about it, then?"

"I expect you to find out from the bus company whether the girl was on the bus, or whether they had a ticketed empty seat. If she was on the bus, I expect you to find out whether she made it to a taxi at the bus station. If she made it to the taxi, I expect you to find out where it took her. I expect you to get further details from the aunt and the girl's parents. I expect you to get photographs and—"

"All right, all right. I know how to do my fucking job."

"If you know how to do your job, Jack, why call me to tell you what to do?"

While he was at the internal phone, Powder made some calls. The first was to the Gun Analysis Office. There, they had finished work on the ballistics test done in Gun Registration on the handgun Aurora Jane Doe had failed to kill herself with. They were satisfied that it was not a gun they were looking for. The weapon itself was still with Gun Registration.

There, Powder learned it had been recently purchased, new. The name on the license application was Sheila Smith. The address given was 3852 North Main Street. Powder took the name and address of the store it had been purchased from.

Finally, Powder called Fraud.

He gave them details from the insulation leaflet he had received from Uncle Adg. He asked for information about the company.

* * *

Mrs. Woods, noticeably deflated, was back in Missing Persons fifteen minutes after Powder finished speaking to Fraud.

"Not going very well then?"

"They say yes but they do no," she said. Her shoulders drooped under her dark shawl. "That mean no Marianna. They not do something. She gone."

Powder reviewed Mrs. Woods's story and promised to follow the matter up. She listened to him but with little faith and no enthusiasm.

When Mrs. Woods left, Powder turned to Agnes, who was engrossed in a record card and the display screen of the computer terminal.

"Agnes?"

"Yessss." She drew the word out to preclude interruption before she was finished what she was doing.

Powder waited.

Then he asked, "Have the bodies come in today?"

"None today. But a lot of these places leave it till afternoon. So there may be some later."

Routine notification of unidentified bodies around the state happened daily.

"Put this description on a match-up list. Anything close, I want to know about." He gave her the description Mrs. Woods had left of her niece.

Agnes studied the details immediately. "May be a murder, eh?" she asked happily.

"You are too optimistic," Powder said sourly.

"But maybe?"

"What is a nice girl like you doing with such a taste for blood? Don't your parents fight enough at home?"

Agnes turned to the keyboard.

"I'm going out for a while. If anyone wants me, I'm on

the firing range teaching Fleetwood quick draws from a wheelchair holster, all right?"

"OK, Lieutenant."

"And don't forget to notice if somebody comes in. If you don't pay attention, they'll steal the rubber plant."

The gun taken from "Sheila Smith" had been sold fifteen days before at a downtown store called Home of Sport.

The owner remembered selling the gun.

"We don't get that many women buying stuff in here," he said, seeking to be chatty with the policeman.

"She gave you a false address," Powder said.

"She did? No kidding!"

"Thirty-eight Fifty-two North Main Street."

"Yeah?"

"There are only two Main Streets in town. One at Fort Ben Harrison and the other in Meridian Hills. They both run east–west. Did you check her driver's license?"

"She said she didn't drive."

"What identification did you take? Let's see your log."

"Come on, Lieutenant. Don't make a meal of it. She came in here, sober and educated . . ."

"And carrying cash."

"That too. But nervous. Very, very nervous. I started on the routine, but she was surprised when I say she needs ID, and she begins to shake and cry."

"Why?"

"She says she's living alone and she's scared. She got back from a couple days away and her place is burgled. It's blown her mind, how somebody from the outside can just bust in. And I know how she feels. I got broke into a couple of times. It's the personal intrusion. So I sold her the gun. She was crapping in her pants about if it happened again and she was there."

Powder shook his head. "In this line of business, and not suspicious of someone without ID?"

The man shrugged. He asked, philosophically, "Tell me the worst; who'd she kill?"

"She tried to kill herself."

"Man, what a relief. I was scared, the way you was talking, I thought she'd topped somebody. I'd have been in hell's trouble then."

"You're in trouble now," Powder said.

Powder used the store telephone to report the man to Gun Registration and got one of their inspectors to agree to check the store weapons register later in the day.

After he hung up the phone, the man said, "Jesus, now why did you have to go and do that?"

"Because the gun you sold her didn't work and I hate rip-offs."

Powder was out nearly an hour altogether. When he returned, Agnes told him that a Lieutenant Gaulden had come around and would be back at three. Fleetwood was not in the office. It was ten to twelve.

Powder had only a couple of minutes to think about what he should do next.

A woman whose sixty-year-old husband had been missing for ten days came in at twelve-fifteen.

"He had fits when he was younger," the abandoned wife told Powder. "Not lately, but when he was younger, he had these fits and he'd take hisself off sometimes for a week. That's what I thought it was this time, but he never been gone this long. Seven days, most, before. Usually four or five."

By twenty past, Powder had wrung from the woman the concession that the "fits" had borne an association with drink.

"Not now, though," she insisted. "He's been dry as a

busted pump since Kennedy was shot. Shocked his handle off, that did."

After asking her husband's approximate height and weight, Powder showed the woman the photograph of the unidentified corpse in County Hospital.

The woman paled visibly.

"Is this your husband?"

"I . . ." She began to shake. "He didn't have no beard." The corpse had several days' growth.

"That sometimes makes it hard to tell. Look at the eyes and ears."

The woman closed her own eyes and passed out.

Carollee Fleetwood returned to the Missing Persons office shortly after twelve-thirty.

"Hey Fleetwood! Guess what! The chaplain knows how to revive women who've fainted. Part of the training they give them these days. What do you think of that?"

Fleetwood couldn't think of anything to say.

Powder said, "I'm glad to see you back. Hold the fort, will you? I want to go upstairs and see somebody."

Fleetwood watched him leave, astonished that he could walk out after making such a palaver about sending her with William Weaver.

Powder stopped first at Fraud, where he gave them Uncle Adg's insulation leaflet and requested, formally, a check on the company.

Then Powder went to the fourth floor to look for Detective Sergeant Jack Greenwell.

Greenwell was a thin man, but with a markedly round head. When he saw Powder standing at his desk, he didn't recognize him. "Yeah? What can I do for you?"

"I want a progress report."

"A what?" Greenwell put down his pen.

"I'm Leroy Powder. Glad to meet you, Jack." Powder

stuck his hand out and Greenwell shook it, formally and by reflex. "And I'd like to know how things are going on the Marianna Gilkis disappearance. I sent the girl's aunt up this morning. You remember. Mrs. Woods. So, what's happening?"

Stiffly, Greenwell said, "Nothing is happening, Powder."

"Oh? Why is that?"

"Because I went to Captain Graniela and he agreed with me that there were insufficient grounds to open it as a case."

"Graniela," Powder said. "My, my. That's a pretty big gun to protect yourself from a little tiny case with."

"Yeah, funny, funny," Greenwood said. "And captain also tells me this story about how there's a nut case somewhere downstairs who spends his life bitching about how his section isn't as important as it ought to be and how nobody understands police work the way he does. So this guy, he spends all his time wasting other people's time."

"Gee, sounds like a real sorehead, Jack," Powder said. "Thanks for the help."

Fleetwood was on the telephone when Powder returned to the office.

He went to his own phone, called the bus station, and asked for the station manager.

"This is Lieutenant Powder, Indianapolis Police Department."

"Yes, Lieutenant. What can I do for you?"

"I need you to check some records urgently."

"All right," he said without hesitation. "I hope I can help."

"A bus from Chicago was due in last night at ten past seven."

"Yes."

"Number one: any unclaimed luggage? Number two: on the passenger manifest, was there an unaccounted absence?"

"You're looking for somebody, right?"

"Right. A woman who traveled from St. Paul and transferred at Chicago. Perhaps you could check the same things on the bus she was supposed to make her connection from."

"I can do that. Glad to help, Lieutenant."

Powder gave the man his number and extension.

One day he intended to have a telephone number of his own, listed in the White Pages along with Homicide and Robbery, Gambling and Vice, and Auto Thefts. Then he could just say, "It's in the book."

Powder saw that Fleetwood was staring at him.

"What are you looking at, kid?"

"What was all that about?"

"Don't let's talk about me," Powder said, exaggerating a stare back at her. "Let's talk about you."

"He's still going camping?"

"Leaves Friday. He says they bought the tent specially and the site is paid for. McCormick's Creek State Park. He's already arranged his employees' schedules. So he's going."

"And comes back . . . ?"

"Sunday night."

"Rather than go camping with William G. Weaver, Junior, would you run away?"

"No," Fleetwood said. "But I would roll away."

Powder rubbed his face.

"No clothes left?"

"Virtually none. Yet the house is packed with bric-a-brac. Shelves of little figurines, pictures of the two of them, mementos of all kinds."

"How many people does he employ?"

"Two were there today. There is a third. I have their names, addresses, and phones."

"And a sense of success or of hard times?"

"It all looks pretty prosperous," Fleetwood said. Then, "Look, if you are suspicious of Weaver, why don't you send the case upstairs?"

"Upstairs?" Powder asked dismissively. "To that bunch of inertia mongers? To get them out of their chairs, you got to drop a body in their laps."

Fleetwood raised her eyebrows.

Powder said, "Last time I took a case up there, guy ran to his captain for permission not to take it. What do you think about that?"

"Sorry I asked."

"Besides, who says I am suspicious?"

"I say you're suspicious," Fleetwood said. "You are asking the questions which one would ask if one were suspicious."

"Ah," Powder said. "But that's different." He paused. " 'One,' huh?"

Fleetwood shook her head. "I'm used to more straightforward people than you, Powder. Guys who say what they mean, if they mean something."

"I didn't ask you how many men had propositioned you recently."

"More than you'd think."

"I didn't ask."

"Can I go to lunch?"

"Let me ask you a question. You're leaving home, right? You pack everything you own, just about."

"Yeah?"

"Why do you leave the china owls and the souvenir cigarette lighters?"

"I had the feeling that she had taken everything that she owned by herself, and left the rest."

"By herself. That helps."

"It does?"

"The checkbook. I've been worrying why she would take all the personal papers and the credit cards but leave the checkbook. But the answer is that it was a joint account."

"I think I'd take the checkbook," Fleetwood said. "It might come in handy."

"OK," Powder said. "Take the checkbook." He took it out of the file and pushed it along the counter to her. "The last three stubs were written the day before the woman left. Talk to the people she gave the checks to."

"Me?" Fleetwood asked.

"I'm not giving orders to myself."

"It's going to take me a while."

"I've got a while. Good practice, rolling yourself around. How did you get along this morning?"

"I managed."

"There you are," he said. "All that department money spent on fancy wheelchairs and car modifications must be worth it."

"Every single cent came from contributions while I was in hospital," Fleetwood said angrily.

"And here you are on your first big Missing Persons case. Got to make the kids' hearts warm that broke open their piggy banks for you."

"I didn't ask for it, Powder. But I'll take help wherever I can get it."

He dabbed at an eye with a finger. "I'd lend you a hanky, only mine isn't back from the laundry yet."

12

*L*ieutenant Gaulden, the officer in charge of police personnel assignments, appeared in Missing Persons shortly after three.

"Hello, Powder. On your own?"

"Yes," Powder said. He finished a report form slowly. Then he rose from his desk to face Gaulden across the counter. "Busy as hell," he said. "Absolutely swamped."

"You have a secretary in here, don't you?"

"Only part-time. I beg her to stay on into the afternoon, I offer to pay her out of my own pocket, but the poor kid is so shattered from all that she has to do in the mornings that she can't face any more."

"That's the one who takes computer classes in the afternoons, isn't it?"

"When she's up to it," Powder said. "But can I ask you what you want? I don't mean to be impolite, but I am really up to my ears."

"I stopped in to see how Fleetwood is getting along."

"Fine, just fine," Powder said.

"Where is she? At physiotherapy?"

"She doesn't have time for that in working hours. Too busy. She's on a case."

"Outside?" Gaulden asked sharply.

"We don't miss many people inside the department."

"We agreed that she wouldn't go out," Gaulden said.

"I don't think we did," Powder said slowly. "You said, 'Of course she won't be able to do much outside the office.' That isn't agreement."

"I explained why we assigned her to you when the appointment was confirmed," Gaulden said. He waved a finger in the direction of Powder's nose.

"You said she was immobile and ought to be somewhere like Public Liaison. But I find that she gets around pretty well. And," Powder continued, warming to his theme, "considering that you gave me the choice of a full-time secretary and no other help or continuing with Agnes and getting Sergeant Fleetwood, I think I'm coming out of your shortsighted, Missing-Persons-is-shit deal pretty well. I need an all-day secretary and three full-time cops to make this service one to be proud of."

"Stow it, Powder. I don't decide manning levels."

Abruptly Powder stopped. "I would love to continue this discussion with you, but I've got too damn much work to do. Good-bye, Gaulden."

"You haven't heard the last of this, Powder. Fleetwood could do this force a power of good, if she would think of the team instead of selfish preferences."

"You mean by trading on pity for the rest of her working life? I wasn't all that certain before, but it doesn't sound like much of a contribution the way you sell it."

Fleetwood looked pale and tired when she returned to the office. Powder watched as she worked herself into position behind the counter. "You look terrible," he said. "Take a load off your feet."

The telephone rang, so Powder didn't hear Fleetwood's response, if any.

The call, from County Hospital, was to inform him

that the woman who had fainted in Missing Persons in the morning had just decided that their unidentified corpse was *not* that of her missing husband.

"You can't win them all, Cedric," Powder told the administrator.

Then an angry bald man in a red shirt walked in.

"Missing Persons?"

"So it says on the door," Powder said.

"Well, I'm missing somebody and when I find him, I'm going to kill him."

"You want Homicide. Kill him first, then go upstairs to the fourth floor."

The red-shirted man took a cigarette out and tapped it on the counter. "Smartass, huh?"

"I said to kill him, not me. You want to smoke, go out in the street."

Powder and the man stared at each other in what was suddenly a test of wills.

No contest. The man put his cigarette away. "Goddamn public servant, huh?"

"What can we do for you, sir?"

"I got a tenant. He's crapped out on me and he took a TV set and my video with him. I want him found."

"Burglary is upstairs too."

"I know," the man said.

Powder frowned.

"I went to Detectives. They said that the kind of information I have on the guy wasn't going to find him."

"Yes?"

"So this cop said, 'They don't have a lot to do in Missing Persons. Try down there.'"

"Did you get his name?"

"The cop? Naw. Little guy, head like a tennis ball. Kind of a little fur all over. And no taste in clothes, this guy. Brown shoes with gray slacks."

Powder took details.

The tenant had been in the room for only a month and the red-shirted man held an extra month's rent in advance.

"I'm not completely out of pocket, but it's the principle of the thing. Guys shouldn't be able just to disappear with TV sets and videos, you know?"

When the office was empty again, Powder turned his attention back to Fleetwood.

"So, what the hell is wrong with you?"

"Nothing," she said.

"You look like you been out all day but you're not strong enough to cut it, that's what you look like."

"I said nothing. All right?"

"Gaulden was in here a little while ago. He wants you in Public Liaison. What do you think of that?"

"It's supposed to be a newsflash or something?"

"I told him forget it. She's too bad-tempered to do PR. That's what I told him. So, see? I'm on your side."

"Thanks."

"Tell me about the check stubs."

Fleetwood leaned her head on one hand for several seconds. Then she bestirred herself and found her notebook. "Three stubs," she said. "One for cash at the bank—"

"Anybody remember her there?"

"I had them trace the teller. But she doesn't remember the transaction."

"All right."

"One stub was at Ayres. Downtown. She bought a large nylon travel bag and she told the sales assistant that it was for her husband."

"The hell she did!"

"She said he was going on a business trip, that day, and wanted her to get a new bag for him."

"That day being Friday?"

"That's right."

"And the third check?"

"Train ticket."

"From Union Station?"

"No. A travel bureau in the neighborhood of the store. Ticket to Washington."

"D.C.?"

"Yes."

"And the same story about buying the ticket for her husband?"

Fleetwood nodded. "It wasn't the first time. She'd bought tickets for her husband's trips half a dozen times this year."

"Well, well," Powder said. "And did you ask Weaver about all this?"

"No," Fleetwood said, looking at him sharply.

Powder picked up the phone and called William G. Weaver, Jr.

"I'd like to ask you a couple of questions," Powder told him.

"Do you want me to come in again?"

"No, no. Now on the phone is fine." Powder could picture the man's expressionless face waiting rigidly with the receiver pressed against his ear.

"You haven't heard anything from Annie, by the way?"

"No."

"Oh," Powder said. "Now, she took money out of the joint account on Friday."

"Yes."

"My colleague ... you remember her?"

"The young lady. Yes."

"My colleague has also learned that your wife bought

a train ticket to Washington, D.C., and a traveling bag, both on Friday."

"Did she now?" Weaver said calmly.

"Yes. The thing that I wanted to check was this. When Annie bought the ticket and the bag, she told the sales people that she was buying them for you."

There was silence at the end of the line.

"Mr. Weaver? Are you there?"

"Yes, I'm here."

"Did you ask your wife to buy a ticket and a bag for you?"

"Certainly not."

"But you had asked her to make traveling arrangements for you in the past?"

"She bought tickets for me. Never a bag. I didn't need another bag."

"And where do you go on these trips?"

"Various cities."

"As far away as Washington?"

"Once to New York, but usually closer. Chicago, Cleveland—"

"And what is the purpose of the trips?"

"I go to conferences and exhibitions. The field of security systems is developing very quickly and I have to work hard to keep up with what is happening."

"I expect you've been sitting rather nervously by the telephone since Annie left, Mr. Weaver."

"Uh, I've—"

"In case she contacted you. Surely that's more likely to happen even than our finding her."

"Perhaps."

"You don't expect her to call, then?"

"I have decided that if she did all this, she is not about to change her mind in a matter of a couple of days."

"I understand that you are getting away from it all this weekend."

"Yes. I told your young lady."

"Camping. Right. I hope you have an enjoyable time, Mr. Weaver."

"Thank you." Weaver paused. "Is that all, Lieutenant?"

"Yes. Good-bye, Mr. Weaver."

Powder put the phone down and rubbed his face with both hands.

Then he turned suddenly to Sergeant Fleetwood. "It's nearly four-thirty," he said. "Why don't you call it a day, kid?"

Before she could say anything, the telephone rang. Powder answered it.

The manager from the bus station said, "I tried you earlier but it was busy. I couldn't keep calling."

"Quite all right. What have you found out?"

Rather proudly: "I can say, for sure, there was no unclaimed luggage on the bus that arrived here or on any possible connecting buses from St. Paul. The head counts on those buses worked out, clear back to St. Paul."

Powder thanked the man extravagantly.

After Powder hung up, Fleetwood asked, "What was that about?"

"When a member of the public helps you out, it's good PR to make a bit of a fuss over him."

"I meant . . ." she began. "Oh, forget it."

"Why are you still here? I thought I told you to go home."

"I am being met after work," she said. "But thanks."

"Don't 'thanks' me, kid. The way you look, you remind me that I'm going to die one day."

Fleetwood said nothing.

"What's that call about?" Powder asked rhetorically.

"It's about that somewhere, in this fair city, there is a niece who didn't make it to her auntie's."

"Oh."

"Do something useful. Call the cab companies and get a list of who picked up female fares at the bus station last night between seven and nine. Women alone or women with men. And where they went. Once you've got that, start tracking back through the drivers and find one who saw a woman of this description." Powder took the description of Marianna Gilkis from the missing niece's file and slapped it down in front of Sergeant Fleetwood.

She was still on the telephone at five when a nervous, muscular man of about thirty hesitated outside the door and then came in.

"We're closed," Powder said. "Come back tomorrow."

The man stood without speaking, and Fleetwood finished her call.

"This is the man who is meeting me, Lieutenant," she said. "Mark Capes, this is Lieutenant Powder."

"Capes," Powder said. "Capes. Wasn't that the name of the guy you jumped in front of to take the bullet that landed you in that chair?"

13

*B*ecause he intended to go out again, Powder parked in front of his house. He walked along the side and went to the garage.

At the garage's side door he stopped. An Indiana Bell lineman's truck was parked in the alley.

"Hey! Dad!"

Ricky was up a pole that stood at the edge of the shed next to Powder's garage.

"I'll be down in a minute," Ricky called, as if assuaging a nervous father's fears. "I just have to make the final hooks."

Powder entered the garage and took down two rolls of garden wire from a considerable stock on a dusty shelf. He also picked up the drawer he had repaired.

He walked back to his car. He put the wire in the trunk, then took the drawer to his neighbor. He went to his kitchen, where he made some coffee.

Shortly after the coffee was ready, Ricky Powder walked in, carrying gloves under his arm and looking mightily pleased with himself.

"Coffee? Great!"

Powder poured two cups.

"You have any sugar?"

Powder brought a bowl of brown sugar from a shelf.

"Hey, I don't mean to be a bother, Dad, but do you have any of the old-fashioned white stuff? This has a funny taste."

"Brown is all I have," Powder said.

Ricky sniffed. He spooned some in.

"What were you doing out there?" Powder asked.

"I put a phone in my room, so I can make calls without it costing you."

"Oh," Powder said.

"Ma Bell has a little spare capacity she won't miss."

"I see."

"Hey, it doesn't mean I'm going to stay forever. I just like to put a phone in wherever I'm in residence more than a day or two. I don't have many talents, so I like to use what I've got."

"You have talents," Powder said suddenly.

"All right. Skills. I don't have many skills."

Powder said nothing.

"Just because I'm living here doesn't mean you're going to lecture me again about dropping out of college, does it?" Ricky asked aggressively.

"Who's lecturing who?"

Powder rose and moved his coffee cup to the sink draining board. "I'm off for a while," he said. "Don't get the police out if I'm late."

Powder drove to a plot of land he owned on the northeast side of the city, just off Alisonville Road, a low-lying section of a former field where he grew things.

Over a period of years he had created a complex patchwork garden with a well-established orchard, unusual flowers, vegetables, and soft fruits. There were also three tiny buildings, housing chemicals, tools, and clothes.

Powder changed clothes and worked for two hours,

splitting his time between making a wire framework ready for asparagus ferns later in the year and hoeing some ground where there were no weeds. He was not a man to let a little work stand between him and what he wanted to see accomplished. If you hoe where there are no weeds there will be no weeds.

At eight he packed up. In one of his sheds he toweled down and changed back to nongardening clothes.

At a quarter to nine Powder arrived outside the house that corresponded to the home address on Fleetwood's file. It was a tiny single-story prefab, off College just south of the river.

He rang the bell and stood patiently outside the door.

"Who's there?"

"Leroy Powder, Sergeant."

"Who?" But the question was more of surprise than failure to understand.

When Fleetwood opened the door she asked, "Whatever do you want?"

"That's not very sociable, Sergeant. Invite me in."

Powder sat in a lightly upholstered chair that was one of a pair in the joint living-dining room.

"I would have guessed you'd be living with parents or relatives," Powder said.

"And now you see that I'm not," Fleetwood said. "What is this, an inspection? Making sure that I'm not faking, that I don't live in an apartment at the top of six flights of stairs?"

"You have no reason to be impolite," Powder said. "I was passing by and I dropped in. That's all."

Fleetwood's face expressed her disbelief.

"All right, I'm a liar," Powder said easily. "I was thinking about one of our cases and wanted to talk to you about it."

"I'm having a little trouble absorbing this," Fleetwood said.

"Too fast for you? Sorry. Have you got a beer?"

"There's one in the icebox."

Powder stayed in his seat. "Guests have to serve themselves? A house rule?"

Fleetwood brought him a can of beer.

"I was thinking about this woman who is trying to keep the world from identifying her until she gets a chance to kill herself. Did I show you that file?"

"No," Fleetwood said.

He told her about Jane Doe Aurora Sheila Smith in between sips of beer.

"I find it hard to find an alternative hypothesis to that which says she cut her face because I threatened to spread her picture around."

They sat quietly for a moment.

Powder said, "So there is someone who might not be hurt as much by her disappearing as by knowing that she killed herself."

"Sounds like parents or close family."

"Mmmm," Powder said.

"Powder, what is so important that it can't wait till the morning?"

"I hoped you would be intrigued," he said.

"What?"

He sighed. "Kids these days need everything spelled out. I want you to go talk to her in the morning. Since you're a slow roller, I thought I'd better let you start off from here. County Hospital, fifth floor."

"And what do you want me to do?"

"Just talk to her. Make friends with her. There's no way she's going to crack in a hurry, but I'm probably too gruff and rough for someone in a delicate condition."

"Your sudden discretion surprises me."

"Any more beer?"

"Look, is this a social call or a business call? I still don't see what's so important that you had to stop by tonight instead of waiting for office hours."

"OK," Powder said. He rose. "I'm on my way. I'll leave you to the *Starsky and Hutch* reruns."

At the door he turned to her. "But the only way you're going to last is as a better cop than the rest of us. And to be better you use whatever hours on the clock are handy. You may not realize it yet, but you're lucky. You got me to work for."

"How lucky can you get?" Fleetwood asked, as Powder closed the door.

14

*P*owder came in early to see if he could extract some information about Uncle Adg's insulation leaflet.

But he didn't get a chance, because three red slips in his message box demanded that he go to the detectives in Homicide as soon as he arrived.

Powder put the red slips in his pocket and went downstairs to prepare for opening Missing Persons.

Agnes Shorter appeared ten minutes ahead of time and Powder worked out with her what routine work should be handled that morning.

Brightly, Agnes informed Powder that she now could use their computer to get into the American Legion's newsletter mailing list.

"Groovy," Powder said.

"I've got this friend in class who helps them out over there. It was just a matter of working out the right numbers so that our computer can unlock theirs."

"You can't get into cab company records with that thing, can you?"

"This what Sergeant Fleetwood is working on?"

"You know about that?"

"There's a draft report here," Agnes said. She began leafing through papers in her receiving tray. "I don't think cab companies use computers yet," she said. "But I can try."

"Never mind," Powder said.

Agnes shrugged.

"What about tapping into the Open Case file to see if you can find a pattern of thefts from rented rooms. Short-stay places. Things like televisions and video recorders."

Agnes made notes on a pad.

"If anybody wants me, I'll be in Homicide," Powder said.

"Homicide? Hey, is something up, Lieutenant?"

"I think they're overworked and want us to take on some cases for them."

In Homicide and Robbery with Violence, Powder sought out Sergeant Bull, the name on the red slips. He had a thin neck supporting an overlarge head and looked like he could only have been out of high school a couple of weeks. Powder had never seen a detective look so young.

Disgustedly, Powder waved the slips at him. "What's so important?"

"Got a body. I want to know if you got any possibles, 'cause I'm having trouble with the ID." Bull pushed an open file across the desk. "Discovered yesterday evening. Female Caucasian, age hard to tell. Fifteen to forty-five. DOA. Body burned, probably after death. Autopsy today. Only partial prints, no joy."

"Where was it found?" Powder asked.

"Scrubland beside a farm road, off Mills Road. Southwest corner of the county. Near Antrim, West Newton."

"So you don't know how long the body had been there?"

"Week or less."

"And from me you want a match-up with the Known

Missing file? Pretty wide open on fifteen to forty-five. I don't see the height or the weight here. Picture?"

"Not much left to photograph," Bull said. "Autopsy was due to start at nine. Details to you when I have them."

Fleetwood was in the office when Powder returned to Missing Persons. His face showed his surprise, but he said to Agnes, "We are looking to identify a woman before they do upstairs. Her body was found last night in a field. See how many we've got with connections in the southwest corner of Marion County, or in adjoining counties—Hendricks, Morgan, Johnson. Any age."

"OK, Lieutenant."

Powder turned to Fleetwood. "Now, you," he said belligerently. "What are you doing here?"

"They didn't want to allow visitors."

"And?"

"So I only talked to her for a few minutes."

Powder looked at her.

"Don't hassle me, Powder," Fleetwood said. "I haven't got her name."

He shrugged.

"I don't understand what business this woman is of ours."

"The hospital asked us to try to identify her," Powder said. "What's her face like?"

"Bandaged, but I talked to a nurse who says they've worked on it to minimize scarring and that a little cosmetic surgery will clean it up pretty well."

"So tell me about the woman."

"She found it hard to talk."

"When she overcame the difficulty, what did she convey?"

"That," Fleetwood said pointedly, "she wants to be left alone."

Powder sighed histrionically. He began to turn away but then said suddenly, "Something I forgot to ask last night. About this guy Capes."

"What?"

"He was your partner?"

"Yes."

"And he's out of the force now, right?"

"Yes."

"It's unhealthy."

"I don't know what it has to do with—"

"He was a cop, and now he isn't. He can't face it. He looks at you and he looks back and he wishes what happened didn't. Guys who look back, who want you to look back, they're no good to you because they're no good to themselves. You get that piece of wisdom for nothing."

Bull telephoned the preliminary autopsy findings shortly before eleven.

The time of death was set as probably forty-eight to sixty hours before discovery. Which made it the Sunday night or Monday morning. The most likely age of the victim was between twenty and thirty, height about five feet five, weight in the vicinity of a hundred thirty-five pounds, race white, hair brown, eyes brown.

The dead woman had had sexual relations not long before her death, and showed mild bruising on unburned parts of her body. No bones were broken. She had never borne a child. There were no distinguishable birthmarks or scars.

Cause of death was a heart attack. The burns on the body had all occurred after death. The pathologist found no additional factors contributing to the death, although a number of laboratory tests were being performed to screen for various drugs. The blood alcohol level was nil.

"Problem is damned cause of death," Bull said. "Heart attack. Not murder."

"You sound disappointed," Powder said.

"My first body," Bull said. "First in charge. But probably just somebody screwing some guy she shouldn't. And, goddamn! she dies! Could happen to anyone, eh? He doesn't know what to do. The usual mechanisms of deception all messed up. Panics. Doesn't see why he should get in a lot of trouble when he hasn't done anything wrong. Maybe too right, eh? Only thing he thinks about is not being caught, only it isn't us he's afraid of."

"Sounds conceivable," Powder said stiffly. "But setting fire to the body? And what about the bruises?"

"Doesn't have to be assault," Bull said.

"What are you going to do?"

"Oh, try for identification. Hope for a lead. I haven't written it off, but I'm not optimistic. If my theory's right, her relatives might contact you."

Powder said, "I'll send up details from my records on everybody who might fit."

When he hung up he said, "I don't like the bruises."

Fleetwood and Agnes both turned to face him.

"Sergeant," Powder said to Fleetwood. "Please liaise with Ms. Shorter and assemble a list of every missing white woman on our books between fourteen and forty, five four and five six, who hasn't had a baby but does have all fingers and toes."

Powder rubbed his face.

He continued, "Agnes will list the file numbers. You pull them. Good to get familiar with our records. Did I ever tell you about the time I located a missing kid because I recognized him on the street?"

"No."

"He'd been gone for seven weeks, and I saw him on the

corner of Sixteenth and Central. Made his mother so happy, I can't say."

Fleetwood watched as Powder picked up his telephone.

"Get a move on," Powder said before he dialed. "What's the matter? Your wheels need pumping up?"

He called Mrs. Woods and explained that a body had been found that might, conceivably, be that of Marianna Gilkis.

"You want me look," she said.

"Yes. It is in Marion County Hospital."

"No use," Mrs. Woods said.

"Why not?"

"I not know Marianna, not from twelve years of age."

"Is there anyone in Indianapolis who does know what she looks like?"

"Not here. St. Paul, her momma."

Powder thought.

"Serious, huh?" Mrs. Woods said. "How this body die? Murder?"

"From a heart attack, but the body was hidden and disguised."

Mrs. Woods frowned. "Disguise body? Funny clothes?"

"Someone set fire to it."

Mrs. Woods made a sound of distaste.

"Not very nice," Powder said.

"You want me get sister?"

Powder thought. "We are trying to identify the body in other ways, and it may well not be your niece. If those identifications don't work out soon, then we'll see about bringing in someone from St. Paul."

After hanging up Powder sat at his desk and stared into space.

Agnes interrupted him by offering a few sheets of paper.

"What's this?"

"That stuff about whether the guy with the missing TV and video is a pattern. I worked out how to extract the information from the central computer."

"What you got?"

"That there have been five TV sets and three videos stolen from rented accommodations in the last eleven months."

Powder leaned back.

"Other things were taken from three places. Couple of appliances and some cash."

Powder gave the sheets of paper back to her. "OK. Get it ready for me to pass on to Burglary."

Powder took the internal telephone and called the Forensic Lab. Yes, they were doing the tests for the autopsy on Bull's body.

"Good," Powder said. "Preliminary report said she'd had sexual intercourse shortly before her death."

"Or shortly after," the technician said somberly.

"What I want to know is, could it have been with more than one man?"

"Christ, Powder, what kind of case is this?"

"A suspicious one," he said. "Can you tell?"

"Possibly. May have to go back to the body, though."

"Do that little thing for me, will you?"

"Why you? It's not your case all of a sudden, is it?"

"I'm cooperating with Bull. Just being, you know, helpful."

The story about the burned body made late editions of the morning paper, the *Star,* and before noon Missing Persons began receiving telephone calls.

"It's like this every time," Powder told Fleetwood.

"Seems to remind them somebody's missing that they forgot about."

Powder called William G. Weaver, Jr., at his store.

"Hello, Mr. Weaver. Lieutenant Leroy Powder here. I wanted to know whether you had heard from Annie yet."

"No, I haven't."

"Sorry to hear that," Powder said.

Weaver paused. "Was there something else?"

"Yes. I thought the department might have called you already this morning?"

"The police department? No."

"Well, you know how it is. These things take time."

"What things?"

"We have an unidentified body of a woman who might be your wife."

"You have?"

"You should go to County Hospital's morgue and have a look."

"Now?"

"Sure," Powder said.

Powder hung up and leaned back in his chair. Then he rocked forward and jumped up. "Enough of this telephone fiddling," he said.

He took Agnes's papers on the television and video thefts and delivered them personally to Burglary.

And then he stopped in Fraud. While he waited, they found out that the company that had printed the insulation leaflets that disturbed the Lockerbie residents' association was registered and properly constituted, as far as they knew. A sergeant called Drayton tried the number on the sheet. "Huh! Weird sound." He shrugged at Powder.

"That all you going to do for me?"

"What do you want, Powder? We're busy here, you know."

Powder returned to the Missing Persons office and

tried the number himself. All he got were funny sounds, not like a disconnection but as if there were a slight fault. Damp connections?

He turned to Agnes. "How good are you at getting addresses to go with phone numbers, kid?"

Powder left the office and the building.

He went to Johnson's store, intending to talk to Uncle Adg about the leaflet. But when it came to the point, he decided that he didn't have anything to say. He did some shopping instead and drove home to drop it off, following a blue Triumph TR7 along Vermont Street.

It pulled up in front of his house.

As Powder parked behind the Triumph, Ricky got out of the car in front of him.

"Hey, hi, Dad. How do you like it?"

Powder stepped forward to examine the vehicle. He went to the driver's side and opened the door.

"You want a drive? Go on, take a spin."

"There's eight thousand miles on the clock."

"It has some time left. You'll be safe enough."

"This yours?"

"Sure. Man, I've always wanted one of these English sports jobs. And the guy offered me such a good price that I couldn't resist it."

Powder took his shopping into the house.

Fleetwood was still on the telephone when Powder returned a little after one.

"There were so many calls, I kept the office open."

Powder nodded and told her to take her lunch break.

"All right," she said.

"How you doing on the taxis?"

"I'm not."

"Well, get on it this afternoon," Powder said.

The telephone rang.

Powder moved to answer the phone, then said, "Hey, hang on a tick."

She stopped.

The call was from Cedric Kendall at County Hospital. He told Powder that the woman who had looked at the corpse of the unidentified man with the beard had come back for a second look at the body and had decided that it was, after all, her husband.

Kendall expected Powder to be surprised.

"Why?" Powder asked. "Half the time they think it *is* who they're missing and then they faint when the missing person walks in the door at home with the loaf of bread he went out for in the first place. People look different dead."

"But her husband!" Kendall said.

"You're the one that's married, Cedric. You ought to understand that kind of thing."

Powder turned to Fleetwood when the call was finished. "Just a minute," he said.

He moved over to Agnes, who was absorbed at her desk. On a slip of paper he wrote out a request for her to check the history of ownership for Ricky's TR7.

"Now," Powder said to Fleetwood, "Jane Doe in the hospital this morning."

"Yeah?"

"What do you think about her?"

"What?"

"What's your feeling about her? Your impression?"

"Troubled," Fleetwood said.

"What kind of troubled? What do you *feel* about her, damn it? What words come to mind?"

Fleetwood didn't know exactly what kind of game Powder was playing, but she offered, "Trapped?"

Powder rubbed his face. He repeated, "Trapped." Then he said, "Good. What kind of trapped? Could it be criminal?"

"You mean . . . ?"

"I mean," he snapped, "could it be criminal trapped? No money to get away, parents live around the corner and read every detail of the newspapers?"

Fleetwood thought, but shook her head slowly.

"Involved in drug and/or violent crimes as a minor participant, say, because of a passion for a major participant?"

"Sort of a Svengali relationship?"

"Who? I was thinking, like, Charles Manson. How does that grab you?"

"No," she said. "I didn't have—"

"How about escaping from something more personal?"

"I guess so."

"So you think maybe it's just your basic suicide on the one hand, with a wish to protect someone from knowing about it on the other."

"That feels better."

"So she's savable. If she's thinking of somebody else even when she's setting about killing herself, there is a connection with the outside which is pretty strong."

"Mmmm," Fleetwood said.

"You can tell her, if you want, that if she cooperates now, we'll do everything we can to sort it out quietly."

"I can tell her?" Fleetwood asked.

"You've made arrangements to go see her again, haven't you?"

"Well . . ."

"But maybe you're right. Maybe I should talk to her myself. Give her a little famous Powder bedside manner."

15

*B*efore she left at two, Agnes gave Powder a brief history of Ricky's new car, and an address to go with the telephone number on the insulation leaflet.

The TR7 had been bought new from Vermillion Auto Sales in September by a Rodney Bladon. In May it had been repossessed, and then resold to the repossessors, Commercial Investigations, Inc., a detective agency. They were the last listed owners.

It didn't mean that the car was not now Ricky's, however. There was a delay up to a business week before new registration particulars were logged.

Fleetwood arrived back at the office a few minutes after Agnes left.

Powder said, "About time. I'm bored stiff with phone calls from people who've just read the *Star.* All the rest are yours."

"All right," Fleetwood said, and she positioned herself at her desk.

"Hey," Powder said, "I've been meaning to ask you, what happened with your calls to the cab companies?"

"There should be a report on your desk."

Powder looked.

Fleetwood said, "No, my mistake. It's still here, on mine." She passed the paper to him.

"Thanks," Powder said. He turned to it immediately, and before he was finished with it, Fleetwood was talking to a telephone caller.

Between the hours of seven and eight-thirty the taxi companies recorded eleven fares from the bus-station taxi stand who were women, or included women.

None of the recorded fare destinations was Mrs. Woods's address or an address in her vicinity.

Satisfied that Marianna Gilkis had arrived in Indianapolis, got off the bus and collected her luggage, Powder deduced that either she had made it to a taxi or she hadn't.

While Fleetwood was on the telephone he tapped her shoulder impatiently.

As she hung up, he said, "Track down these women. Find out whether they arrived where they were supposed to."

He waved the report in front of her face.

"And while you're talking to the cab companies, find out whether there were any unusual gaps in the availability of any of their drivers that night, whether they were on the list with these fares or not."

"Don't interrupt me when I'm on the telephone," Fleetwood said sharply, but Powder was already dialing his own phone.

William G. Weaver, Jr., at his place of business, answered saying, "Lock and Key."

"Lieutenant Powder here. Have you been to County Hospital, Mr. Weaver?"

"I have. It wasn't, isn't my wife."

"Are you certain?"

"Certain."

"Why?"

For once, Weaver hesitated over his answer. "What do you mean, why?"

"I gather the body doesn't have a lot of face left."

"No," he said quietly.

"So I wondered how you could be sure that it wasn't your wife. What things made you so positive?"

"It just wasn't," he said.

"Give me a for instance," Powder said persistently.

"The little toes. My wife has small splits on the toe-nails of her little toes. If she doesn't trim them regularly, they catch on her stockings or tights and make holes. The woman I looked at has totally different feet and nails."

"OK, Mr. Weaver," Powder said. "I'll certainly let you know if any other unidentified bodies are discovered in the area."

"Oh."

"You don't sound enthusiastic. Don't you want to find Annie?"

"Of course," he said. "But it was so horrible."

"Suspicious deaths often are," Powder said cheerily. "Good-bye."

As he replaced his receiver, Powder's internal phone rang. The caller was Sergeant Alexander Smith, in Crime Prevention.

"I just wanted to thank you," Smith said.

"What for?"

"That work you did on TV and video thefts. We're planning to circulate all the casual-room-rental establishments to warn them."

"I sent that to Burglary. They were supposed to go catch the guy."

"That's a little hopeful, isn't it, Lieutenant Powder?" Smith asked earnestly. "It's a big city, after all."

"They just passed it on to you?" Powder asked.

"Yeah."

"Not working on it themselves?"

"Gee, I don't think so. But I think it will do a lot of good, especially with the description you included. If a renter spots a possible and gets back to us, we have a fair chance of picking him up."

"Shit," Powder said. He hung up.

About three Powder suddenly stood and said, "Why is nothing happening here?"

Fleetwood, just off the telephone, looked at him as if he were crazy.

"We haven't had a sensible new case all day."

"Do you often get like this?" Fleetwood asked.

"How's your taxis?"

"I think," Fleetwood said, "that I have just about accounted for them. If you assume that the two who were listed for the airport actually got there and intended to get there."

"Accepting that, what are you left with?"

"I'm left with one fare who went to a corner, rather than an address, with a taxi driver who was working his last day."

Powder sat down. "Tell me about it."

"Not much to tell. One passenger, unspecified."

"OK. Check the driver out."

Powder stood up again. He still felt restless.

"Are you going somewhere?"

"You sound like my goddamn wife used to," Powder said. "Yeah, I'm going somewhere."

16

*P*owder's first stop was the morgue in County Hospital. He went to look at the body of the heart attack woman. It was possible that he would be reminded of one of the pictures in his case file.

The body reminded him of no one. The flesh of the face was too badly mutilated.

As he looked at the woman's mortal remains, Powder felt unaccustomedly agitated. Sick of the aggravation in the world.

Dissatisfied with his own life.

He left to go to the address Agnes had provided as a match for the telephone number on the insulation leaflet.

It was a small brick house with paint flaking off the window frames. There were no signs whatever of commercial activity.

Powder rang the bell.

A small woman with a cane answered the door and smiled at him. "Catalog?"

"No, ma'am," Powder said. "I'm looking for the Cozy Hoosier Insulation Company. I understand that they operate somewhere close by, and I wondered if you could direct me."

The woman asked him to repeat the name. She thought about it. Then said, "I'm sorry, young man. Never heard of 'em."

"Excuse me for disturbing you," Powder said.

"That's quite all right. I've found life very quiet lately. A little disturbance makes the day more interesting," the woman said. She closed the door.

Powder drove to the East Tenth Street address given in the phone book for Cozy Hoosier. It was a small administrative office in a street storefront. On presenting his ID Powder was immediately shown in to the boss.

"What can I do for you, Lieutenant?" the man asked nervously. He was short and fat, and as he began to sweat he wiped his forehead with a white handkerchief he took from his desk drawer.

Powder showed him the leaflet. He read it slowly.

Then he read it again.

He looked at the telephone. He buried his mouth in his handkerchief. "Jesus God," he said. He closed his eyes. "The money I paid for that printing!"

On his way back to the department, Powder stopped at Lock and Key.

Although the store did not have a large street frontage, it was very deep and well stocked.

Powder did not see William Weaver. But two young women glanced at each other as he came in and without speaking decided which would assist him.

Powder asked to see Weaver, but as he did so, Weaver appeared from an office room in the back of the store.

The clerk, a slightly built woman in her early twenties, left without comment.

"Hello," Weaver said impassively.

"I was driving this way, thinking about absent wives, so I thought I'd stop in and see how you were coping."

"I see," Weaver said.

"I haven't been here before. Quite a place."

"Thank you," Weaver said.

"You have three employees, I believe."

"That's right."

"Only two here. One has the day off?"

"Yes."

"I sort of expect a security store to have male clerks. Is the third one a man?"

"No," Weaver said. Then, "My wife did all the hiring."

"Oh," Powder said. "That's interesting. And did she do the firing too?"

"When it was necessary. But she has good judgment about staff."

"You must have confidence in them if you are going to leave the store on Friday and Saturday. Pretty busy days, I would have thought."

"Sometimes," Weaver said.

"Who will be in charge?"

"Miss Hilgemeier."

"Which one is she?"

"She's not here today."

"How are you getting along, without Annie? I take it she's not returned?"

"No."

"Or called?"

"No."

Powder waited.

"I'm coping," Weaver said finally.

"I was thinking," Powder said, and then paused to look at the photoelectric door openers.

"Yes?"

"Have you canceled the credit cards which Annie took with her?"

Weaver hesitated. Then he said, "No."

Powder looked him in the eyes. At last, he said, "That's pretty cunning."

"What do you mean, Lieutenant?"

"If it were me, I'd probably cancel credit cards my wife took because I wouldn't want her spending my money. But it's cunning because if she uses them, then you'll have an idea where she's gone."

"I suppose I will," Weaver said.

"Well, much as I would like to stay and gas some more, I've got to be getting on now," Powder said. "See you again soon."

For a few minutes after he returned, Powder worked on the Listing of the Missing, which he distributed monthly to hospitals, travel points, employment offices, housing bureaus, welfare offices, social and community workers, and to other police departments in the Midwest.

Often, work on the Listing was a reminder of his irritation with police planners for their failure to see the advantage of making the document bigger, more frequent, and backed with personal visits by Missing Persons staff.

This time, Powder was less impassioned. When he decided to close the file, he announced to Fleetwood, "With more money, we could get it out every two weeks, maybe find one extra kid."

Fleetwood was dealing with the paperwork from a couple whose foster son had been gone from their home for two days. She didn't have the faintest idea what he was talking about.

At five to five Powder called his ex-wife at her place of work.

"Good heavens. What do *you* want? Make it quick. I can't stay on the telephone for personal calls."

"This is not a personal call," Powder said.

"You know what I mean, Leroy."

"It's about your son."

"Ricky? What about Ricky? Has something happened to him? Is he hurt? What's happened? Don't mess around, Leroy, tell me, for God's sake!"

"He's not hurt."

"What's happened?"

"Nothing's happened," Powder said irritably.

"You wouldn't call me about him if nothing had happened."

"I just wanted to know when you saw him last."

"What's wrong? You're talking about him like you were tracking him. What has happened, Leroy Powder?"

"Nothing's happened. He just seems to have a lot of money all of a sudden. I called you to ask, in a civilized way, whether you made a financial contribution when you saw him last. That's all."

"He's all right?"

"As all right as he ever is," Powder said.

"Always facetious."

"Always," Powder agreed. "Did you give him money, or not?"

"So what if I did?"

"Several thousand bucks?"

"Now where would I get cash like that?" she snapped.

"The question that I want to answer is where *he* got cash like that," Powder said.

"I'm sure that there is nothing wrong."

"Good. Where did he get it?"

"He lived here for about three months, until a couple of weeks ago."

"You're not telling me he opened a savings account with the rent he didn't pay you?"

"No, but he was doing some work on the side with some friends."

"What sort of work?"

"I don't know what sort of work. I didn't pry. But he was working very hard. Evenings, weekends."

"Doing what?"

"I said, I don't know what."

"He's just bought a fancy new car," Powder said. "Any parent would be entitled to ask how he paid for it."

"By working, of course. How else?"

Too involved to allow for the fact that she couldn't see him over the telephone, Powder shrugged.

"Trust him, Leroy."

They hung up.

When he turned to look, he saw that Fleetwood was watching him.

For a moment he stared back. Then he chuckled. "I don't know about you, kid, but I'm beat."

She said, "It's been a long day."

He rose and looked at the log.

They had recorded twenty-three phone calls as a result of the stories in the *Star* and the afternoon *News*. Some had been referred to Bull; two had been opened as new cases in Missing Persons.

"The power of advertising," Powder commented sourly as he turned the inside lock of the front door of the office. "But you already know about that, with your Heart Line Wheelchair Appeal."

Fleetwood, who looked gray and tired, said nothing.

"We'll have another batch tomorrow morning, when the *Star* reports no progress today."

"Did you want me to go to the hospital in the morning?" Fleetwood asked.

"No."

"All right."

"Why put off till morning what you can do tonight?"

17

*W*hen Powder pulled up in front of his house, there was a young man on the porch ringing the bell. Getting no response, the young man seemed uncertain what to do. He carried a shallow, wide cardboard box.

Powder approached him slowly.

"Can I do something for you?" Powder asked.

"What? Oh. Is this where Rick Powder lives?"

"I think so."

"Is he around?"

"I don't know," Powder said.

"Can I leave this for him?"

"Sure."

"Tell him Sal brought it, will you?"

"All right."

Powder took the box and the young man hurried down the front walk and turned toward downtown. Powder watched till he passed out of sight, then held the box up to his ear. He heard nothing.

Powder opened the door and let himself in.

He put his shopping in the refrigerator and carried the box to Ricky's room. There, he penciled on the outside, "From Sal, no carrying charge." He put the box on the bed.

Then Powder searched the room.

The things he found that interested him most were Ricky's checkbook, a large plastic sports bag, a nylon money belt, and a shoulder holster.

The last check stub in the checkbook showed the amount Ricky had sent to register his new car. But that wasn't what interested Powder. There was no stub for a check that paid for the car.

The sports bag contained a variety of items of electronic equipment and several tiny reels of tape. Much of the equipment had the Indiana Bell logo on it.

The money belt held nearly seven hundred dollars in fifties and twenties.

The shoulder holster was empty and looked new.

Before he left the room, Powder looked in the cardboard box. Inside was a dark-tan trench coat.

Powder parked in front of a dusty horizontal duplex on Tecumseh Avenue just north of Michigan. He rang the bell for the lower house. When the door wasn't answered he rang again. Then he knocked.

A woman with streaks of light and dark red hair threw the door open, smiled broadly, and asked, "You been there long? The bell doesn't work. I suppose I should put a sign on it. But that kind of thing is really a landlord's responsibility, don't you think?"

"I suppose so," Powder said. He held up his ID. "I'm a policeman. May I come in and talk to you for a few minutes?"

The woman's smile faltered only for a moment. She stepped back. "Please enter," she said. "Always pleased to cooperate with our men in blue. Even when they're not in blue."

She led him to the door of her living room. She turned, however, and asked, "Would you like a cup of coffee?"

"Yes. Thank you."

They sat in the kitchen while the woman made coffee. "What is it about?" she asked lightly.

"Mrs. Annie Weaver."

After a little thought, she said, "Is that the woman from the lock store?"

"I was under the impression that you were friends."

"Well, we're not enemies," the woman said, turning to smile as the coffee began to brew. "But I hardly know her."

"She is missing from home, and her husband listed you as one of his wife's three friends."

"You know," the woman said, "the other day I had a phone call from a man asking whether Mrs. Weaver was here. I said she wasn't, so he said good-bye and hung up. I thought it was peculiar, but then being a single girl again I get some odd phone calls from time to time. I hadn't given it another thought until now."

"What day was that?" Powder asked.

The woman considered. "Saturday? How do you take your coffee?"

"Black."

"Are you sure? You haven't tasted my coffee."

She poured two cups and gave one to Powder.

The woman asked, "What were the names of the other two friends?"

Powder told her.

"They hardly know her either," the woman said definitively. "I know Mrs. Weaver better than they do."

Powder sipped his coffee. The woman sat down.

"I went into this lock store, you see, to get a lock. I'd been watching TV about making doors and windows secure and it sank in. But I didn't know a lot about locks. So I asked the girl who came to help me, when Mrs. Weaver took me over. She is quite a strong personality and we got chatting. She said she didn't get out much and I suggested that she come along with me and my friends sometime.

We—and you have the other two on your list—the three of us go out to the movies or sometimes to a play, maybe once a month. A meal first, and then a drink or two after. It's a laugh and we generally have a real good time."

"Did Mrs. Weaver go out with you?"

"Only the once. And that must have been nearly a year ago. And she didn't have much fun. It was all right until after the show, but to tell the truth, I think she disapproved of us flirting with the barman and some of the guys who were drinking where we went. After a night out and a drink or two my friends and I get a bit frisky. Nothing serious. Well, except for me. I'm the only single gal, and you never know. But the Weaver woman was distinctly uncomfortable and quiet. And I never heard from her again."

Fleetwood opened the door to the gap allowed by the chain, squinted, and said, "I don't believe this."

"That's not very polite, Sergeant," Powder said. "Invite me in."

Powder sat in the same chair as the night before. "Oh, it's good to sit down," he said.

"You were just passing by again, I suppose," Fleetwood said. She was not relaxed or amused.

"Yeah."

"What is it with you, Powder?"

"What do you mean, Sergeant?"

"Are you after my body?"

"Should I be?" Powder asked. "That good, huh?" He wagged a finger in her direction. "Whatever your own feelings may be, Sergeant, I think you should understand from the beginning that my relationships with people I work with have always been strictly business. Try not to be disappointed."

"I'm tired," Fleetwood said. "What do you want?"

"A can of beer would be nice."

"I'm all out."

"Do you get enough to eat?" Powder asked. "All I've had is a cup of coffee, but then I'm on a diet."

"What?"

"What have you had to eat tonight?"

"I haven't been home long. And I'm not very hungry."

"Shall I make you an omelet? Do you have any eggs?" Powder got up and went to the kitchenette, in a corner of the room demarcated by a curtain rail, though there were no curtains.

Fleetwood rolled after him. "Damn it, get out of there. I'm not hungry. All I want is for you to tell me why you're here and leave so I can have some peace and quiet after a long day."

Powder took a can of beer from the refrigerator. "The young are so impatient," he said reflectively. "Do you want one?"

"No."

He took a second can of beer, opened it, and carried it back into the living section of the room. "Sure you don't want an omelet? It's no trouble."

Fleetwood didn't speak. But she had to take the beer as Powder lowered it toward her lap. She knew he would just drop it otherwise.

Powder sat and took a long drink. "The young are so impatient," he said again. He nodded quietly. "One forgets. You know, Sergeant, I have a son who is not all that much younger than you. Twenty-two. I haven't had him living with me for several years, but he moved in two days ago and I'd forgotten, simple as that, I'd forgotten what it was like to be young."

He paused. Fleetwood said nothing.

But she sipped the beer.

"I'd like you to meet him sometime. I'd like your impression. Because I'm worried about him." Powder drank. "How did you get on at the hospital?"

"Nothing substantive. It's very hard to get through to someone who not only doesn't want to talk to you, but finds it physically hard to speak."

"She'll probably be better tomorrow," Powder said. Suddenly he sat up and pointed a finger at Fleetwood. "Hypothetical question for you. Pretend you are a woman with a bit about you, a touch of class. And suppose at the same time you've got some kind of trouble that you just can't escape from. What, really, is it going to take to make you determined not just to die, but to die anonymously? What is it?"

Fleetwood said nothing.

Powder said, "The humiliation of finding yourself in a situation, even if you weren't at fault for getting there?"

He paused for a moment, but not expecting an answer. "It's just not a pattern you see. Usually they're dying to leave notes, excuse the pun."

Fleetwood began to cry.

A few minutes later she said, "Not that it's exactly the same for me, but you don't know the number of times I've looked at myself in this wheelcage and said, 'That can't be me there!'"

Powder nodded, slowly.

Fleetwood looked at him.

"You bastard," she said. "You sent me to see her to try to get me to use my sob story to bring out hers."

Powder failed to deny it.

"Except that it didn't work. She didn't talk to me."

"Did you cry when you were with her?"

"Are you as coldhearted a bastard as you pretend?"

"Colder," Powder said.

18

Powder was joined at breakfast by his son.

He looked at his watch as Ricky entered the kitchen. He held it to his ear. "Must be slow," he said.

Ricky rubbed his cheeks, then slapped himself with both hands. "Got a long day today," he said. He poured a bowl of Cheerios and drenched it with sugar and milk. He sat in front of his cereal and then didn't eat it. "Dad?"

"Yeah?"

"I talked to Mom last night."

"How is she?"

"Fine."

"Great?"

"Pretty great. Look, she says you talked to her yesterday too."

"I called."

"But you didn't tell her I was living here now."

"She didn't ask."

"Don't you think that's pretty childish? She doesn't feel this competitive thing about me, so you not telling her means that you're playing games with her."

Powder looked at his son. "That's all you talked about?"

"You can't say it's none of my business," he said. "I

can't stand this being in the middle of something stupid. Don't you think it's about time you grew up?"

"You go first, kid. Show me how."

Powder stopped at the travel bureau where Annie Weaver had bought her train ticket to Washington the day before she disappeared. He identified himself to the chubby white-haired man behind the counter and said that he was doing some routine background work on the disappearance of Mrs. William Weaver.

"We had one of yours in here a couple of days ago asking about that," the man said, his blue eyes gleaming.

"Did you?" Powder asked noncommittally.

"Yeah, gorgeous little thing. Hey, you must know her."

Powder looked puzzled.

"The girl that nearly got killed, day after Christmas. Shot on duty. I recognized her right away. I did. And I'm real glad to see she's back at work, even if it's in that wheelchair. She asked me all about Mrs. Weaver, and did it real nice too."

"I'll have to compare notes with her," Powder said.

"You want to ask too, huh?"

"Just one or two things."

The man smiled broadly. "Suspicious circumstances? That's what it is, huh? You suspicious of this guy, Weaver? Funny guy, I always said."

"How's that?" Powder asked.

"Just . . . funny. No expression on his face. I always said to Sandra, you could kick that guy Weaver in the balls and you wouldn't be able to tell it by his face."

"Who is Sandra?"

"My girl that works here." The man looked at his watch. "She oughta be here by now. Always late, Sandra." He sighed heavily.

"Do you know Weaver well?"

"Naw, not really. Except you know the other commercial people in an area. By sight. At Christmas-decoration meetings. That sort of thing."

"Have you met Weaver?"

"A few times. I been in his store. And he came here about a month ago."

"What about?"

"He wanted information about campsites in state parks."

"Could you help him?"

"I told him to buy a state map. They got that kind of thing on them."

"And that's the only time he was here?"

"Yeah," the man said, "definitely."

"So his wife bought the tickets for his trips?"

"That's it; always by train."

"And always the day before he was to leave?"

"No. Usually the week before."

"But this last time it was the day before?"

"That's right. And she was mad as hell about it too."

"About what?"

"Having to rush around for him because he decided to go away after all."

"And she bought only one ticket?"

"Yeah." The man was puzzled.

"All right," Powder said, putting his notebook away. "Thanks."

"That's all?" the man asked.

"That's all."

"The lady did it a lot better. The one before. She thought of lots more stuff to ask. Good little woman, that. Wish she was working for me. I told her that, when she was here. I did."

"What did she say?"

"Not to be surprised if she took me up on it."

"Yeah?"

"Yeah, no kidding. Turns out she just got assigned to a new branch, or whatever you call it."

"Section."

"Yeah, section. And the guy in charge is some kind of nut. She called him a troglodyte."

"A what?"

Proudly the man said, "Troglodyte. It's fancy talk for how the guy can't cope with the way things are in the twentieth century. I looked it up."

Although Powder arrived some ten minutes before the office was due to open, Agnes and Fleetwood were already there and two people were waiting outside the door.

"Morning," Powder said cheerfully. "Carollee, get the information on the taxi fellow, will you?" he asked as he gave Agnes a slip of paper that asked her to get the annual income of Richard Henry Powder and details of any outstanding debts to banks or loan companies.

Powder was about to open the office when the telephone rang.

He was required in Homicide immediately. He went immediately.

Bull was waiting at the elevator door. Powder wished he'd walked up the stairs.

"What's so urgent?" he asked.

"This. Forensic supplement on my burned body."

"So?" Powder asked.

"They say the woman had had sex with at least three different men shortly before she died."

"Or after," Powder said.

"They say you asked them to check that. Why?"

Powder looked at the young man. "You seem suddenly more concerned about this case," he said.

"Afraid I've screwed up," Bull said. "Didn't take it seriously and lost time. Made me think again about the bruises," Bull said. "Consistent with rape."

"Mmmmm," Powder said. Bull understood that Powder agreed that he had dismissed the case too quickly.

"I'm getting an artist's impression of what she might have looked like, for the papers and TV. Need to identify her, and wondered if you had any leads or ideas, Lieutenant."

"Happy to help if I can," Powder said.

"Thank you," Bull said earnestly.

"But all I have is what I sent up before. Most likely from those is a young woman from out of town, traveling alone, by bus, who got to Indianapolis but didn't get to the place she was supposed to. We've established there's a cab driver who picked up a fare at the station at the right time and took the passenger to a nonspecific address. It was the cabby's last day on the job and he didn't ask for a reference when he left. His home phone is a rooming house he no longer lives at. Cabbies are entitled to leave their jobs and move. But it's the only thing approaching a lead I happen to have."

"I'll look into it."

Powder walked down the stairs and back to the office.

Which had only Agnes and Fleetwood in it.

To the assembled pair he announced, "I respect a cop who admits a mistake and who asks for help. Damn few of them around."

Without waiting for the observation to start a philosophical discussion he said to Agnes, "Got something else for you to do."

"Shoot."

"I want you to look through the IPD computers for women who have disappeared from bus stations, train stations, airports. Then the same for state police and, if you can get it, for nearby big cities. But start here, over the last five or six years."

"Any other parameters?"

"Parameters? What is it, big-word day or something? What the hell is 'parameters' supposed to mean? Fleetwood?"

Fleetwood looked up.

"How you doing, CF?"

"OK."

"In that case, I'll leave you to it." Powder left the office.

At County Hospital he found that Sheila Smith Aurora Jane Doe was spoken of more sympathetically than the last time he had come to see her.

He told her so as he sat down beside her bed.

"They're all right here," she said.

"You remember who I am?" Powder asked.

"Yes."

"Sergeant Fleetwood asked me to send you her best wishes. She might have come herself, but she's been having some trouble on the job."

"I'm sorry to hear that," the woman said with some hint of feeling creeping into her otherwise colorless voice. She seemed to be able to speak without pain.

"Yes," Powder said. "Fleetwood is quite a person."

The woman nodded slowly.

"It's about time we knew who you were," Powder said. He looked at her matter-of-factly.

"I've been thinking about that," the woman said slowly.

Powder waited.

"But I can't tell you."

"Is it because I am a policeman?" Powder asked.

"Only a bit."

"At least we are not playing at not knowing who we are," Powder said.

"No," the woman said quietly.

"You are a moral responsibility for me," Powder said.

"How is that? Like the Chinese thing about having to take care of someone you save? It's all right. I'm a big girl. And you haven't saved me."

Powder looked interestedly at the woman. "I read a little about China once," he said. He sighed. "I'm far too sensitive to be a policeman. But I feel that it does the force good to have some round pegs for their square holes."

The woman was silent. Powder felt she was thinking about Fleetwood.

"There is nothing I can do, of course," he said. "There's no way I can make you tell me who you are and what your problem is, even though Fleetwood and I would like to help."

"There is nothing you can do." The woman's eyes became grave.

"I can do one thing."

"What?"

"You are clearly desperate that you do not become publicly identified, living or dead."

"Yes," she agreed.

"I can promise that if you kill yourself, I will publicize your original face in such a way as to make it virtually inevitable that whoever you don't want to know about you finds out."

The woman said nothing.

"It is a promise," Powder said.

"What business is it of yours!" she screamed. "Leave me alone!"

19

Powder stopped at Mrs. Woods's house. He didn't know whether to expect to find her at home, but she was there and her face showed immediately the lack of pleasure his arrival brought to her.

They exchanged no greetings. Mrs. Woods said, "Bring sister, yes?"

"I think it would be as well."

"I phone."

"Although, before you do, might there be some point to your looking at this woman? It's just possible you would be able to identify her one way or the other."

Powder drove her to the County Hospital morgue.

"I not know," Mrs. Woods said after she had studied the body.

Powder just nodded.

On her way back to the house he asked, "What was Marianna intending to do in Indianapolis?"

"Live," Mrs. Woods said.

"I mean, get a job? Or study?"

"Get job, when can."

"What sort of job would she have been looking for?"

Mrs. Woods turned to him. "I do not know. I not know

girl good. But you talk like she dead. You know this and not say?"

"I don't know what has happened to your niece," Powder said.

"Talk like you do," she said.

"I don't mean to."

When Powder dropped her off, she said, "I call sister now. Then call you."

"Good," Powder said, and drove away feeling respect for the matter-of-fact way with which this person approached life.

For the first time in a long while he thought about his mother, an immigrant to Indianapolis from southern Missouri. During her shorter-than-average span, life and death were what mattered to her. While accepting the latter she applauded actively the things that encouraged the former, without ever worrying seriously about the frills most people spend their time on. Powder felt he owed her a lot.

When he arrived at the office, Fleetwood was being shouted at.

"Don't just sit there," an irate man was saying. "Do something."

"You!" Powder said. "I mean you!"

The man turned. He was accompanied by four people: a woman and three prepubescent boys.

"What?" the man asked aggressively.

"Keep your voice down or get out," Powder said. "If my sergeant weren't such a compassionate person she would probably have had you thrown out already."

The man still looked angry.

Powder said, "There's a bell we use for disruptive members of the public. She taps it with her foot and three big guys come running. If she's called them, you'll be lucky to get out of here by next week. Tapped your foot yet, Sergeant?"

"No."

"That's a close call for you, mister," Powder said. "Now come in here, and tell me what your problem is."

The whole group trooped into the interview cubicle.

Powder sat behind the small desk and let the family sort out among themselves who got the three chairs.

"So, what's happened?"

"This is what's happened," the man said. "Sixteen years old and we get up one morning and find this."

He waved a piece of paper around.

"Give it to me and keep quiet while I read it," Powder said.

The note said, "I'm gone to live with Jack. Don't try to find us or we'll just go somewhere else. Love, Natasha."

"She's left home to live with her boyfriend?"

"Sixteen years old," the man said. "Go arrest the little bitch!"

"Horace!" the mother said. "Language!"

"Sorry Phyl," the man said. He explained to Powder, "I'm just so blankety-blank mad."

Powder looked at him. "She still in school?"

"No. She left two weeks ago."

"So you want her arrested?" Powder's eyebrows rose.

While the man hesitated, the woman said, "We've been up to the social work. And they won't make Nattie come home. So we've come to you so you could tell her, if she don't come home she'll go to jail. That's what we want, isn't that right, Horace?"

"That's just about the short of it," the man said.

"We don't know where she's at, so you'll have to find her first."

Powder said, "If I find her *and* some law's been broken, she'll be jailed."

"You can't just warn her to come home?" the mother asked.

"No," Powder said definitively.

"We pay good taxes. It's a terrible example she's setting for the boys here. What if they go astray? Preventative, I call it," the father said.

"You want me to find her?" Powder asked harshly. He took a form from the drawer of the desk.

The couple looked at each other. "I don't know," the woman said.

Powder sighed and put the form away. "You think about it. If you want to involve the police, you come back, hear?" He stood up.

Powder appeared behind the Missing Persons counter when the family had left the office. Fleetwood said, "What do I do with this long form I began filling in for them?"

"Throw it away, my dear. Throw it away."

She threw it away. "I was handling it," she said clearly.

"Insecure bosses have to interfere sometimes," Powder said lightly. "Makes them feel important. Now go to lunch."

She went to lunch.

Powder looked over the log. The entry that caught his eye was a visit by the young man Burrus, who had reported his girlfriend as missing on the day Fleetwood had started work. The disheveled man who had come to the office at the same time as William Weaver. The girlfriend sighing in the bathtub.

Burrus had come in to ask what progress was being made.

It reminded Powder that he wanted to call Weaver.

"Mr. Weaver?"

"Yes."

"Lieutenant Powder here."

"What do you want, Lieutenant?"

"Have you heard from Annie, by the way?"

"No."

"Pity. Couple of things. First was, is there any insurance on her?"

"On . . . my wife?"

"On Annie."

"What kind of insurance?"

"Life insurance?"

"She has a small life policy."

"How much for?"

"Fifteen thousand dollars."

"What kind of policy?"

"Thirty-year term."

"And when did you take it out?"

"When we were married. We both did."

"I see. Thank you. The other thing was to ask what time you would be leaving for your vacation tomorrow."

"In the morning. Early. I'm not sure what time."

"So if I want to see you, it had better be today."

Weaver seemed to sigh. "That would be the more convenient."

"Bye now," Powder said.

Agnes, who was not in the office when Powder returned, came back at about a quarter to one. She carried some case files.

"I thought you'd gone," Powder said.

"No, no," Agnes said. "I've been tracking down your travel-naps for you."

"Oh yes?"

"I've got the three incidents in the file here in Indianapolis and I've lodged requests in Fort Wayne, Lafayette, Evansville, Cincinnati, Louisville, Columbus, South Bend, Chicago, and Toledo."

"Tell me about the three in Indianapolis."

"I can't," Agnes said. "I've got to go, or I'll be late for class."

Powder read through the files.

Two of the three incidents had occurred before his time in Missing Persons, though none of the cases had gone through the office.

Five years before, a forty-year-old woman returning home by bus from a visit to relatives had not arrived. She had been on the bus and her car, which had been left in the bus-station parking lot, had been collected and driven away. The car was found later, abandoned in the southeast part of the city. Nothing more had been heard of the woman.

A year later another woman traveling alone had disappeared from Weir Cook Airport. She had had no car and police were told by her father that she had planned to take the bus into the city. She was twenty-six at the time. Her decomposed body was found seven months later in an empty house in Terre Haute, Indiana.

The third incident had also happened at the bus station. A nineteen-year-old woman en route from Kokomo to Evansville had been accosted by a man in a trench coat who pressed a gun into her side and told her to keep quiet and come with him unless she wanted to be killed on the spot. The woman had screamed and run, and the man had fled. This incident had taken place on an early evening the previous July. The man had not been identified.

Powder closed the office and went upstairs to copy the files. He put the copies in an envelope addressed to Bull, delivered the envelope to Homicide, and then went out.

He walked up to Twelfth Street, where he looked in the windows of a couple of costume companies.

On the way back he stopped for lunch in a salad bar and became engrossed in making doodles on the paper napkin.

Fleetwood had already opened the office by the time Powder returned.

"Hey," he said. "What did the guy Burrus want?"

Fleetwood looked up and said, "Didn't I record it in the log?"

"Yeah, but what did he *want*?"

Fleetwood sighed and ran her hand through her hair as if trying to muster the energy to deal with unraveling this one of Powder's games.

Powder said, "He was told that we wouldn't be looking actively for his lady friend. So what does he *want*?"

"He wants her trussed up and returned in manacles. How do I know?"

"Still as dirty looking as he was the first time?"

Fleetwood said, "He certainly didn't look any too appetizing."

"Mmmmm."

"One thing he did say. That he might be going to a private detective."

"Pity I wasn't here," Powder said.

"Why's that?"

"I could have recommended one."

"Do we have a list of recommended private investigators?" Fleetwood seemed interested. "It's just I have a friend, but I didn't know whether to mention it."

"No. This would have been unofficial. Anyway, my acquaintance is probably out of business by now." Powder looked at her. "You know a private eye, huh?"

Fleetwood said nothing.

"This wouldn't be the recently retired Detective Capes, would it?"

Fleetwood shrugged.

"Sergeant."

"Yes?"

"How the hell did you end up taking a slug for Capes? What's the story?"

Fleetwood inhaled sharply.

"A boyfriend, was he?"

"No," she said quietly. "He wasn't. He was married."

"But he's not now?"

"Almost not."

"A boyfriend now?"

"No," she said.

"What kind of duty were you on?"

She looked at him. "Do we have to talk about this?"

"Yes," Powder said.

"We were on the ground, staking out a meeting of some armed-robbery suspects."

"On the ground?"

"There was an alley in the back. No easy vantage point, so we hung around *in* it."

Powder frowned.

"We hung around, as if we were a couple making out. He had his arms around me, hands on the guns in the back of my belt; I had my arms around him, hands on the guns in the belt at his back. I also had a small repeating weapon hanging from my neck and it was damned uncomfortable and we were giggling about it and pretending to cuddle while we were keeping watch. And then, for a moment, we weren't pretending, and that was the moment that something went wrong at the other end. One of the suspects came out the door, shooting. I pushed Mark off and pulled a gun and I don't remember a lot after that."

"Did they catch the guy?"

"Not then. Mark emptied at him, but he got away. They caught up with him the next day and killed him."

"I see."

"Happy now?" Fleetwood asked him, staring rigidly at his face. Powder saw how much effort it had cost her to talk with such apparent ease about the incident.

"Yeah. Great," he said.

She straightened the papers on her desk. "I'm going out," she said.

"Oh. OK." Powder said. "Great." He turned to routine work of his own and only looked up after she had left.

Powder closed the office late. He stopped at home and then drove to William Weaver's store. It looked empty. He banged loudly, insistently, on the door. There was no answer.

At Weaver's house the bell was answered quickly.

"Oh. Lieutenant Powder."

"I told you I would be coming," Powder said. "But I left it late because I wanted to have a look at your house."

Weaver did not make way for him at the front door. He stood mute for a few seconds, as if deciding whether to say anything.

"Have you heard from Annie?" Powder asked.

The question tipped the balance for Weaver. He shook his head tensely. He stepped back into his hallway and held the door open.

Powder strode in, looking at all the trimmings. Powder carried a sports bag and casually turned to Weaver and said, "One of the things I wanted to see you about was this." He passed on the bag, which he had taken from Ricky's room.

"What about it?"

"There are various items in it which reminded me of things I saw in your store. I wondered if you would have a look through and tell me what the stuff in there is used for."

Without eagerness, Weaver said, "All right."

"OK if I have a look around while you do it?"

Again Weaver hesitated, but he said, "Feel free."

Powder walked quickly through the rooms. Downstairs he felt the working of an unusually fussy hand, with color coordination in each room going beyond paint, paper, and furnishings to include the profusion of small decorative trinkets Fleetwood had noted.

Upstairs there were two bedrooms. One was used as a study and all that Powder really looked at in either was the closets, where he found only men's clothes and not many of those.

The spacious garage was attached to the house. There Weaver's preparations for his camping trip were evident. A sleeping bag and air mattress, what appeared to be a very large tent, a kerosene lamp, and a can of kerosene were laid out on the top of a large chest freezer, ready for packing.

Powder thought about clearing the freezer top for a look inside, but instead he passed on to prod a sack of cement and two larger sacks of sand that stood next to a couple of shovels on the back wall.

He satisfied himself that the sacks contained what they were supposed to, and not Mrs. Weaver.

William Weaver was waiting for Powder in the hall.

Powder said, "I talked to one of your wife's friends yesterday."

"Oh?"

"She said that she hadn't seen your wife for nearly a year."

Weaver stared silently.

"Does that surprise you?"

"Yes," Weaver said.

"Why's that?"

"My wife said she went out with the three of them."

"How often?"

"About once a month." Weaver paused. "Could it be that the woman you spoke to had not been going out with the others?"

"No," Powder said. "It couldn't. Looks like your wife was telling you fibs."

Weaver said nothing.

Powder picked up Ricky's bag. "What's the stuff in this, then?"

"There appears to be equipment for working with telephones, although some of the tools are for more general use."

"Working with telephones how?" Powder asked.

"Well, recording from them."

"Bugging?"

"Yes."

"Sell a lot of that sort of thing, do you?"

"It is part of the current scope of my business," Weaver said.

"OK," Powder said. "Thanks." He took the bag.

Weaver seemed about to speak, but Powder left.

He sat in the car for several minutes. Then he drove to his garden on Alisonville Road.

Despite a long physical session Powder felt tense as night drew in. Edgily he changed clothes and, on his way back to town, where Alisonville Road ran into Keystone, he stopped at a supermarket.

When he pulled up outside Carollee Fleetwood's small house, Powder found a car already parked there.

Fleetwood answered the door, saw who it was, and said, "I already have a visitor, Lieutenant."

"That's all right," Powder said. "He or she can stay. I don't mind."

The visitor was Mark Capes.

"Hello, Capes," Powder said, sitting down. "How's the sleuthing?"

"Fine," Capes said. "I'm enjoying it a lot."

"Carollee here didn't say who you work for. Or are you a noble lonely seeker of truth for a fee?"

"I work for Commercial Investigations."

"Well, well," Powder said.

"You know it?"

"Indirectly. They do some repossession, don't they?"

"Some," Capes said. "But I've been brought in to take charge of their personal-inquiries side. They think there's a big future there, as a supplement to the work done for commerce. I'm developing it for them."

"Divorces and that?"

"The range of work is very wide," Capes said stiffly. "The only restriction on what I can take on is that it's done for individuals rather than for companies. It's a real thrusting, forward-looking outfit and I'm pleased to be aboard."

"Hey," Powder said, "I got a hypothetical situation for you. Test your powers of reasoning."

"Come on, Powder," Fleetwood said.

"No, no," Powder said. "We'll see how good a gumshoe he is and maybe put him on our recommended list." He turned back to Capes. "See, you got this lady married to a guy that owns a store. And she works in the store three days a week, but she is at home three days when he is in the store. He's the most controlled and routine guy in the world, so when he's in the store, she knows he's going to stay there, know what I mean?" He winked exaggeratedly. "On top of that, the guy goes away overnight maybe every month. I'm not going too fast for you, am I?"

"Go on," Capes said.

"OK. That's the situation. Now what I want to know is, with all this free time—did I say, there are no kids and nobody else at home?—with all this free time, what I want to know is why this gal would have to make up a story that she was going out with girlfriends now and then, when she wasn't really going out with them at all?"

"I give up," Capes said. "Why?"

"No, no. You don't get it at all. You got to tell me why. Because I don't know. Why's she got to lie?"

Capes shrugged.

"Ah well," Powder said. He leaned back. "Capes, you were a triple-citation man in your first four years in Detectives, weren't you?"

"Yes."

"Why'd you pack it in?"

"What?"

"Couldn't you face Fleetwood here rolling around in a chair for life, or were you just afraid that the next time nobody would be there to step in front of you?"

Capes paled.

"Leave him alone, Powder!" Fleetwood shouted. "He's an invited guest in my house, which is more than you are."

"Nobody can run away from facts," Powder said. "You know that better than either of us, since now you can't run away from anything."

Capes stood up, and said, "I've got to go, Carollee."

"Don't you dare leave!"

The man looked indecisive, but said, "No, really. I'm on assignment."

"He's an ill-tempered, bad-mannered bully, just like everybody says. He'll be gone in a minute. In fact, he's going now."

"I've got to get back. Honest."

Capes left.

When they were alone, Fleetwood said, "Go away, Powder. Go away!"

"So you can cry in your beer in peace? No, I wouldn't do that. Besides, this time I've brought the beer."

From a brown paper bag Powder took a can of beer. He opened it and sat down on the table next to Fleetwood's wheelchair.

With a wild sweeping gesture, she knocked the can flying across the room. It hit the inside of the front door and crashed to the floor where its contents poured out.

Powder looked in his bag and pulled out the other can of beer. He opened it. "Have you eaten?" he asked.

Fleetwood said nothing.

"Because I haven't. I bought this pizza when I got the beer. You mind if I put it on? There's plenty for both of us, if you want some too."

Fleetwood said nothing.

Powder went to the electric grill and put the pizza on.

"I don't generally eat this frozen stuff," he explained. "But this doesn't look bad, as they go."

While it cooked, Powder sat again, and sipped his beer.

"What's the matter with you?" Fleetwood asked bitterly. "You got no place else to go at night?"

"I'm pretty busy," Powder said. "Please don't become dependent on this attention. It won't last forever."

"That's something, I guess," Fleetwood said.

"You know," Powder said, "I was walking around a while after work and I got reminded of one of the things I like best about summer."

Fleetwood stared at him.

"In the early evening, when the day has cooled off a little, you walk past a building and you can feel heat on your arm. The sun shines on the stone and it holds the heat for a while. Then you walk past and feel it. I really like that. It reminds me there is warmth in the world, you know? It's one of the things I like best about summer."

Powder got up and took the pizza from the grill. "Doesn't take long if it's thawed," he explained. He cut it in half and served the pieces on the top and bottom of the box it had been packed in.

"Whole-meal base," he explained. "Good stuff."

He ate silently and drank a little beer. "Hey, I'm not being polite. You spilled your beer. Here, have some of mine." He put his beer down on the table next to Fleetwood. He finished his pizza.

Sitting back, he said, "That was good."

Fleetwood did not touch her food.

Powder put his hands behind his head and said, "You know, sometimes I see guys like your friend, Capes, who obviously don't mind much whether they're in the police force or not. I mean, fine, nobody likes a partner to take a slug, but in my day, not even just me, but in my day generally, if that happened then the guy would just go out and get six citations where before he would have only gotten three, so that the partner's slug would be worthwhile. But nowadays, it gets uncomfortable for a guy and he just packs it in. I don't understand how people can do that and still get up in the morning.

"I didn't want him to quit," Fleetwood said.

"Course not. But you're more like a real cop, aren't you? Still, if that's the way he's made, maybe it's all for the good. It's a funny old life, ain't it, Sergeant? You're the one everybody wants to quit, but you won't."

"You want me to quit too, huh?"

"Me? Naw. I'm all for having you kill yourself trying."

"Pleasant of you to offer such support."

Powder looked at his watch.

"Christ," he said. "It's late. I'd love to stop and jaw with you the rest of the evening, but I've got things to do.

What I came by to tell you was this. Tomorrow night there will be some duty time in the evening from about eight, so you can take the afternoon off if you want to."

Fleetwood was suddenly interested. "What's it about?"

"I'll fill you in later. Nothing dramatic. Nothing to jump in front of bullets for, but I don't have the time to tell you about it now."

Fleetwood shrugged.

Powder stood up. "I'll leave you alone while there's still some night left. All right?"

Powder picked up the can by the door and set it on a window sill. Stepping around the beer on the floor, he made his way out.

Powder stopped at a bar two blocks from his house. He joined two men from the neighborhood whom he recognized. They talked about displays of temper in sports. Powder defended the younger generation. After his first two beers he began to add bourbon chasers.

20

*P*owder rose very early. Quietly he made coffee and filled a vacuum flask. He drove to William Weaver's house, where he parked across the street and waited.

Weaver opened his garage door at seven-fifteen. He backed his car out, closed and locked the garage door, and then drove off. Powder followed.

His interest was whether Weaver picked anyone up before he went for his camping trip, but Weaver drove directly to Kentucky Avenue, which ran southwest into Route 67, the road to McCormick's Creek State Park. Powder followed as far as Valley Mills. Then he turned around and drove to his office.

Midmorning Agnes gave Powder details of Ricky's salary, a copy of his last bank statement and current balance, and the information that Ricky had no outstanding loans from commercial sources.

Around noon, Sergeant Bull came to the Missing Persons office to tell Powder that he had located the missing taxi driver, who had a room in a small boarding house. The man had been in debt and under financial pressure, and he had driven cabs at night as well as holding a day job to ease the situation. Bull would be interviewing him shortly about the case of the partially burned body.

Powder thanked Bull genuinely for keeping him informed.

In the middle of the afternoon, Powder tracked down the telephone number of the manager of the McCormick's Creek State Park's campsite. He called the man, identified himself, and asked whether Weaver had arrived.

"Yes, sir," the man said. "He checked hisself in this morning."

"Was he alone?" Powder asked.

"He was alone when he got here, yes, sir."

"And now?"

"I ain't saying it's different now. He's at the far end of the site, about as far away as he can git, and I can't say as to whether he's still alone there or not."

"Is he where he is because you're full, or by choice?"

"We're pretty busy, but he picked his spot out when he booked it."

"He booked the site in person?"

"Yes, sir. I recall it clear as the sky is blue. Kinda fussy fella. Wanted a site just so. Right size, right kind of ground, not too close to neighbors, that kind of thing."

"When did he book it?" Powder asked.

"I can look the date up if'n you want me to."

"Yes, please."

The man took two minutes to find that Weaver had booked the site eleven weeks before, in the beginning of April.

"You seem to remember him pretty clearly," Powder said.

"I do. I don't do full-time on the campsite here till first of May, but I got other duties around the park. He come and found me where I was, working on one of the bridges on Two Mile Trail. Fella made me leave what I was doing to sign him in, this one particular spot."

"Did he say why it had to be that particular place?"

"He said it was gonna be his wife's first time camping and—" the man stopped himself. "Hey, that's funny."

"What?"

"That he ain't got his wife with him, after all that fuss and bother."

"I take it," Powder said, "that usually people don't request specific sites."

"Oh, sometimes they do. Like, when they been with us before and liked it. But I had the impression with this fella that he'd been doing the rounds before he got here."

"What kind of rounds?"

"Other parks. He said Shakamak when I asked where he'd come from. I was expecting him to say Indy or Muncie. A city or town, you know?"

"So it's a good site he picked?" Powder asked.

"Funny thing," the man said. "I wouldn't have said so. It's a distance from the, uh, facilities, and it's a little low and tends to catch water if it rains a lot."

"I see," Powder said.

"Anything else I can do for you?"

"I'd be grateful if you'd have a look at him from time to time, see if his wife shows up, that kind of thing."

"Sure. Glad to," the man said.

Half an hour before closing time, Powder turned from his desk to address Fleetwood about how on a Friday he usually reviewed the week's work but this time he didn't feel like doing it because of the strain of having to break in a new section member.

Only she wasn't there. Took the afternoon off.

Powder laughed at himself momentarily.

*   *   *

When Powder got home, Ricky, fresh out of the shower, came into the hall to meet him. He dripped on the hall carpet.

"Hi, Dad."

"You're home early," Powder said.

"Getting ready for the party tonight," Ricky said. "Do ... you remember?"

Powder eyed the towel. "That your costume?"

Ricky smiled and widened his eyes as if with drama. "I'm going as a private detective."

"Oh," Powder said.

"If you want me, just whistle," Ricky mimicked.

Powder looked sadly at his son. Then he said, "Wait there, will you?"

He walked out to his car, took Ricky's bag from his trunk, and brought it in. "Part of your costume," Powder said, dropping it heavily on the floor. "It was in my trunk. I don't know how it got there."

He left his son in the hall and went out again.

Uncle Adg Johnson was not looking well. He admitted to indigestion.

"You should eat better and less," Powder said. "Get rid of that blubber, feel good."

Johnson was not accustomed to being given critical advice. He said as much.

"Maybe that's why you're so fat," Powder said. "Look. It's the end of the week. I want to clear this insulation leaflet thing, OK?"

"We had a robbery in the neighborhood," Johnson said. "On Tuesday. Did you hear about it?"

"No," Powder said.

Johnson belched uncomfortably, making it seem a commentary on inefficiency in the police force. "Landers.

You know them? They were visiting her mother. Since Sunday."

"I have checked the leaflet," Powder said. "It is on the level. Mistake in printing on the telephone number."

Uncle Adg looked at Powder dyspeptically. "Bit of a coincidence," Adg said.

"But the company did run an ad to get people to distribute the leaflets, and they divided the city into sections. I've got the name of the guy who has been distributing them around here. I can probably arrange for him to get a police visit, but maybe you'd rather look into it and see whether he's just been careless about the way he put the things into the letter boxes. Company's calling all the leaflets back anyway, to change the phone number."

Powder passed a slip of paper with the distributor's name on it to the fat man.

Powder arrived at Fleetwood's at twenty to nine.

He rang the bell and there was a delay before Fleetwood answered the chime. He rang again.

Suddenly the door opened and before him Fleetwood stood, balancing precariously on two aluminum crutches. The wheelchair was immediately behind her, but she stood for seconds, challenging Powder to compliment her.

He didn't speak. So she said, "You said we were on duty from eight."

"I couldn't get my kid out of the shower."

Fleetwood looked at him. "Tie, tiepin, cuff links. Where the hell are we going, Powder? You didn't tell me it was fancy dress."

Despite himself, Powder smiled. "Fancy dress is what it is."

"You want me to change?"

"No. I want you to take a load off your feet."

Fleetwood lowered herself into the chair. It rolled several inches and she dropped one of the crutches.

"Takes practice," Powder said. "This walking. More difficult than it looks. Do you know, technologists working on robots find the mechanism of two-legged walking one of the most difficult problems to solve."

Fleetwood said, "You really don't want me to change clothes?"

"No."

They went down her path to his car.

"Forget about that damn chair," Powder said.

"You can lift me in and then fold the chair in the back."

"Lift you?"

"Don't worry, I'm not contagious."

"Is there an alternative?"

She looked at him to see whether he was serious. "We can take my car."

"Let's take your car."

Once on the way, Powder started talking suddenly about William G. Weaver, Jr.

"I've been harassing him," Powder said.

"How?"

"The question isn't how. It's why."

"You're suspicious of him."

"You said that before."

"You denied it."

"I was wrong," Powder said. "I am suspicious of him."

"Why?"

"In the end, because he reported her missing and he doesn't complain when I call him or see him every day."

Fleetwood said nothing.

"Either he is emotionally strangled and the report of

her missing is his only concession in an otherwise perfect defense against the loss of her departure. Or . . .”

“Or what?”

“Suppose he’s murdered his wife.”

“Why did he do it?”

“Anybody who is married can find reasons for murder. The problems are how, when, and what has he done with the body?”

Fleetwood shrugged again. “You sure she’s not sitting happily in a bathtub somewhere?”

Suddenly, Powder turned on her. “Of course I’m not sure. I’m just being friendly. Speaking my mind on a subject of mutual interest before we get to the party.”

“Party? What party?”

“Just keep driving, will you?”

“What are we going to, Powder?”

“It’s along here,” Powder said, as they turned onto Lockerbie Street. “I’m not sure exactly where, but there should be a TR-Seven parked out front somewhere.”

21

*T*he house was a two-story wooden building with a steep, off-center roof, narrow arched windows, and a portico doorway as ornate as the actual facade material of the house was plain. It was genuine old.

Music was audible from the street but not disturbingly loud and colored splashes of flashing light made it clear that the place was a center of festivity.

Fleetwood wheeled herself to the door in silence. As Powder helped her up the two front steps she said sharply to him, "What the hell kind of police business am I supposed to be conducting here?"

"Just keep your ears open and mix," he said.

"You're a pervert," she said. "You just wanted a date but didn't have the guts to ask for it."

They were greeted by a rooster. "Hello there!" it said. Then studied them. "You, uh, got the right place?"

"Sure do, man," Powder said. "Where's the drink?"

"Great. Great! Down the hall and on the left."

"Cock-a-doodle-do," Powder said. He pushed Fleetwood down the hall. On the left, in a small alcove, they saw a profusion of bottles and glasses on a table. As they arrived at it, a man in blue clothes and blue face paint appeared at the other end. He was accompanied by a bunny girl with blue hand-prints on her chest.

"It's a goddamned costume party," Fleetwood said.

"I told you it was fancy dress. What do you want to drink? Orange juice? Don't forget you're driving."

"Just what the hell kind of costume am I supposed to be in?"

"You've come as a cripple," he said.

The blue man and the bunny looked up at them for the first time. Then left.

"Oh, thanks a lot, Powder. Thanks a bundle. That's really terrifically tasteful. Hundred percent perceptiveness."

"If you'd known ahead what would you have done? Dressed as a Sherman tank?"

"You claimed this was work," Fleetwood said fiercely.

"You're getting time off in lieu. That makes it work, so any problem squaring it becomes mine and not yours."

"Brief me, Powder. Tell me what I am supposed to do? Protect the diamonds on the hostess's kneecaps? Or was it something with the host you had in mind for me?"

He pointed a finger at her. "What I have in mind is for you to keep your eyes and ears open. Meet people."

"Who? Who are you expecting to be here? William Weaver?"

"Check out a guy in a private eye suit for one," Powder said. "Talk to the people who talk to him. Dance. Socialize."

"Scotch and soda," she said.

"What?"

"I want a drink. Scotch and soda."

Powder poured some cola in a glass and then topped it up from the soda siphon. He gave her the glass and said, "Get your own ice, if you want it."

He left her.

* * *

In the kitchen, near a replica Ben Franklin stove, Powder found a partially unwrapped mummy with small ears talking to a pair of pirates. He walked up to her and interrupted the conversation. "Hi, Rebecca. Great party. Thanks for inviting me and my friend."

Rebecca Coffey looked at Powder blankly, but one of the pirates said, "Hey, it's Ricky's dad, the cop."

"Oh yeah," Rebecca said, still looking blank but now more pleased. Powder suspected that her personal party had begun quite a while before.

"Where is the big fella?" the same pirate asked. Powder recognized him as Dwayne Grove, the phone-company accounts and records man in the group that had been in his house. Powder was sure Rebecca was being asked about Ricky, not her husband.

"How you doing, Dwayne old man?" Powder said heartily. He pounded Grove on the back so hard that his earrings rattled. "Who's your friend?"

Grove introduced Raphael McGregor, who broke his silence to take Powder by the lapels and say, "What a suit! What a nostalgia trip! And it looks like it was made for you!"

Powder ignored him to say to Grove, "I hope my son fed you folks well the other night."

"Oh, terrific," Grove said with enthusiasm. "Really took us to the trough and pushed our muzzles in it."

"I'm glad the kid upheld the family reputation for hospitality." Then Powder added with a wink, "Mind you, I don't know how he does it on a lineman's salary."

Dwayne Grove laughed, and offered a conspiratorial smile that excluded the other pirate, who in any case was busy feeling the lapels of Rebecca Coffey's costume and saying, "Nice material, but not authentic Egyptian."

* * *

Powder located Fleetwood talking animatedly to a baseball player sitting on a couch. On the other side of her, a diminutive, hairless Tarzan sat on the floor. Powder saw the Tarzan begin to rub Fleetwood's leg.

He was about to go to her when he saw another of the people who had been to his house, John Hurst, dressed as a Native American, talking to a riverboat gambler Powder felt he had met but could not place.

Powder walked up to the two of the them and grabbed Hurst's hand. "Roy Powder, Chief," he said. "You're Hurst, aren't you?"

"That's right."

"And who's this?"

Powder placed him at the same time Hurst said, "Clive Burrus."

"Glad to meet you, Clive. Nice to see you again, Hurst. Having a good time, I hope? Take care."

Powder left as abruptly as he had arrived and proceeded to interrupt Fleetwood's conversation, which had expanded from the baseball player to include a woman in a tuxedo. "Hey," Powder said, "can I have a word with you, Carollee?"

Fleetwood hesitated, but the Tarzan rose and slid quietly away and Powder pulled her chair a few feet into the space.

"What is it, Powder?"

"Did you know a subadolescent Tarzan has been rubbing your leg for half an hour?"

Fleetwood looked for the Tarzan.

"What's the matter, you don't feel so good down there?"

"I can let someone rub my leg if I like it. What do you want?"

"What I want is to call your wavering attention to another of your assignments here."

"What's that?"

"The guy Burrus that came into the office twice, shabby and dirty. Missing a girlfriend."

"Yes?"

"He's here, in rhinestones and a waistcoat and spats. So, in between bouts in the jungle, I want you to find out who he is, who he's with, what he does. And if you can, something about this missing girlfriend."

Fleetwood looked around for Burrus.

Powder said, "You didn't think this was just a social swirl on IPD time, did you? Don't forget, you're on duty, Sergeant."

He turned her back to the couch, where instead of the ballplayer, Father Time had sat down to rest his weary bones.

The party's music and dancing were centered in a cleared room at the back of the house. Powder watched a while in the doorway. Then he felt a tug on his shoulder. The tugger was Chief John Hurst, who said, "I was very impressed with your comments about food the other night and the way the big corporations sacrifice us little people for the sake of their profits. Thanks."

Powder looked at the man, but did not speak.

A woman dressed as a Pilgrim Mother walked by and Hurst grabbed her by the waist. "Here's another victim of the big corporations, damn and blast them, aren't you, Lila?"

"I'm not Lila," Lila Lee said, slurrily. "As you can plainly see I am Wilhelmina Truscott."

"Who's that?" Hurst asked.

"Who's that? Who's that? That's the problem with you pigs." She looked unsteadily at Powder and giggled. "Sirry sor. I mean, sorry sir. By pigs I am meaning, more generally, pigs of the male chauvinist ilk and not of your ilk, if you follow my drift."

"My sails are full of your drift," Powder said.

Wilhelmina Truscott frowned momentarily and then laughed, "Oh good."

"A victim," Hurst said. "A victim, and as a result she goes and gets sloshed whenever she gets the slightest excuse."

Unsteadily, Lila shook her head. "That's a damn lie. Damn lie. Not so."

Hurst began to speak, but Lila continued. "I don't need an excuse. Not even a slightest one." She laughed, but cut it short to ask, "What do you mean, 'victim'?"

"I mean Terry."

"Oh." Tears welled in her eyes. "Poor Terry."

"Terry," Hurst addressed Powder, "is Lila's husband."

"And what's happened to Terry?"

"He's in jail, that's what's happened to Terry."

"I see," Powder said stiffly.

"The pigs put him there," Lila said, "and this time I mean your kind of pigs."

"Terry was convicted of dealing in cocaine," Hurst said. And he waved a finger in the direction of Powder's face. "Dealing in cocaine *is* illegal and Terry *was* at it, so, superficially, it seems straightforward."

"Yes," Powder said. "It does."

"But my point is, why is it illegal? You seem to be simpatico for fuzz. Why is cocaine illegal? Will you tell me that?"

"No," Powder said.

"Well, I'll tell you. And the reason is the big corporations that have a stranglehold on the alcohol market and they can't stand something that will do for people what alcohol does, only better. They've got too much invested. So they make sure that government sends poor little guys like Terry away forever and a day because they are a threat, *a threat,* to the stranglehold of the alcohol lobby. That makes governments *and* corporations fair game, as far as I am concerned."

"You guys shouldn't take a nice guy like Terry," Lila said, as if she'd been saving it for minutes. "Such a sweet, nice guy that wouldn't hurt a fly."

"I can vouch for that," Hurst said. "The nicest guy in the world."

Slowly Powder said, "You think it's a bad law, right?"

"A stinker. A corrupt—"

"Would you like to know how *I* can help?"

"How?" Hurst asked, for them both.

Powder smiled and nodded gently. "By locking up everybody who even knows how to spell cocaine."

The sudden hard glare in Powder's eyes silenced them both.

"If I, as a police force, come down as hard as I can with a law, that's the way to affect the most people and get them to think about whether it is a bad law. So the best thing for me to do is go out and bust everything in sight. Is either of you carrying?"

"Just a—"

"Thanks for the opportunity of this little conversation," Powder said. "I've enjoyed it a lot."

Powder left them and carried his empty wineglass in the direction of the bar.

At the end of the entrance hallway, Powder saw a trench-coated figure working at unraveling the mystery of the pharaohs.

Powder took his drink to them. "Hi, guys," he said heartily. "Hey, this is the first I've seen of Sam Spade, Junior, here." He slapped Ricky on the back. "Hey, great little party, Mrs. Coffey."

"Uh, thanks," Rebecca Coffey said.

"I'm having a whale of a time. I'm meeting all kinds of people to talk to. Nearly like being at work, only nobody has come even close at guessing my costume, what do you think of that?"

Powder stared at Rebecca, demanding a response.

"Hey, take it easy, Dad," Ricky said. "She isn't used to people like you."

Ignoring Ricky, Powder said, "Go on, take a guess."

Rebecca shook her head dazedly. "Lawyer?"

Powder beamed. "Hey, that's not bad. Not right, but not bad. Hey, since you are my hostess, you are going to be the first to know. What my costume is, is a plainclothes police detective!"

Ricky began to interrupt, but Powder stopped him. "No, wait, that's not all. A plainclothes police detective on detail to track down guys who are doing illegal wiretaps. What do you think of that? Good, eh?"

Rebecca nodded, dazedly again, and Ricky said nothing.

"And you know how I tell them? First, you sniff them out because they're making money, usually in cash, above and beyond the amount that would be expected from whatever job they seem to hold. And having money, easy-life types gotta spend it, so you'll see them with flashy cars. The next thing is that they go around carrying burglary and bugging equipment. A dead giveaway. Take Ricky here."

Ricky looked stricken, but Rebecca was not keeping pace at all, and giggled slightly as she looked at Powder's son.

"He would be the type we're after, only he isn't carrying the equipment. So, there you are. But a great little party, enjoying myself a lot. Is your husband around? I'd like to thank him too."

"He's upstairs," Rebecca Coffey said, "but he doesn't want to be disturbed. He's, uh, with somebody."

"Oh, great. I wouldn't disturb him for the world. But maybe I'll catch him later. What costume is he in?"

"Well, he started as a tennis player but he might be into something else by now," she giggled mightily. Ricky stood stonefaced.

"Groovy," Powder said. He saluted the couple with his wineglass and strode away.

Powder found Fleetwood talking to a penguin, but didn't hear what they were saying. "Come on, Carollee," he said, "They're playing our song."

He rolled the startled sergeant into the music room, where an enthusiastic mass of people, hardly coupled, bounded to the rhythmic music. Powder took Fleetwood to the middle of the floor and started gyrating before her.

She immediately moved toward the exit, but Powder stood in front of her. "You've lost the beat," he said. "Forget your troubles, try again."

Again she strove to leave, but he headed her off. She sat still then, as Powder aped various people he saw around them. The track ended, and Powder rolled her off the floor.

He said, "You're not as tough as you think you are. By the end there I saw you tapping your little finger."

Fleetwood looked up at him and said, "Never do that again!"

"So, you don't dance, huh? You're no fun at all."

He rolled her back to the penguin.

The penguin stood up and said, "You must be Lieutenant Powder."

"Up against the wall and take the position," Powder said sharply. "How do you do?" He shook the penguin's flipper.

"Before your twirl, Miss Fleetwood and I were talking about incarceration," the penguin said.

"Something you know a lot about?" Powder asked chattily.

"Not from first hand," the penguin said. "But I was explaining that I feel there is a lot wrong with imprisonment, and she was in the process of defending her role on society's behalf."

"I'm with you," Powder told the penguin, and he struck a conversational pose.

"You are? How interesting."

Nodding gravely, Powder said, "Current trends and practices are most disturbing. Particularly overcrowding in prisons and jails, and the number of unconvicted people who do time just waiting for trial. It's scandalous."

"I'm very interested to hear you say that," the penguin said.

Fleetwood looked on silently.

"But what's worse is the tendency across the country to take the soft option of a hard line."

"By which you mean?"

"Flat-time sentencing, abolition of parole, and many of the practices associated with juvenile so-called justice. The fact is that group incarceration is a net increaser of crime rather than a protection from it. A comprehensive rethink of sentencing alternatives is the only way out of a spiraling hole."

"If you feel that way," the penguin said, "doesn't it make you hesitate before you arrest somebody?"

"Nope," Powder said. "Get the cuffs on and down to the slammer. Nothing more satisfying. You want a drink, Miss Fleetwood? I'm feeling thirsty." He took her glass and his own back toward the hall.

But instead of refilling them, he carried the empty glasses to the stairs. Ricky and Rebecca were no longer standing at the foot of the balustrade. Powder went up.

On the second floor he found four doors. One, a bathroom, was empty. The other three doors were locked. Powder stood on the landing, puzzled.

He went downstairs and in the front hall he found a stocky girl dressed as a three-star army general.

The girl saw his empty glasses and said, "Shit, you looking for a bottle that's got something in it too?"

"No," Powder said. "I'm looking for someone to tell me why the rooms upstairs are locked."

"Oooo," the girl said. "Naughty, naughty." But then she looked puzzled. "You were looking for a free room alone?"

"What's the drill, General?" Powder asked. "Rooms available for little parties during the big party?"

"That's it. There's keys in the doors on the inside."

"Someone must have taken the list of house rules down from the wall," Powder said.

The girl snorted, and then asked, "What are you dressed as?"

"Well," Powder said. "It's a pretty subtle getup you see before you. A lieutenant of police, dressed in plain clothes, working out of the missing persons section of the Indianapolis Police Department."

The general scrutinized Powder carefully. "Gee, how do I tell?"

"If you look really close," Powder said, "you can tell from the furrows in the brow."

The general looked close.

"It's a rough game, this missing persons. You army types can just go in and shoot people, but we have mothers and lost children, crying their eyes out, when *we* know the children they've lost don't want to come home. That's the real kind of missing."

The general suddenly had tears in her eyes. "That's terribly moving," she said.

Powder nodded, actually affected by the tears he had brought on so facetiously. "It's a taxing, saddening job for a cop who cares," he said.

Through her tears, the general said, "Do you cry about it sometimes?"

Powder didn't answer her at first. Then, compassionately, said, "Not often."

"I cry all the time," the general said. "But this time feels more than usual."

Powder stood and nodded quietly.

The general said to him, "That's a hell of a costume, mister." She wiped her eyes and walked away.

Fleetwood was alone when Powder returned her refilled glass. She looked tired.

Powder sat on the floor beside her. "You stewed?" he asked.

"Sure," she said.

"Your friend Capes," Powder said.

Tightening, she said, "What about him?"

"My guess is that he hangs around you for *you* to comfort *him*. Have I got it right?"

She looked at him.

"Sort of like when a guy's partner gets killed and the guy feels guilty about being the one left alive? Have I hit it?"

She said nothing.

"Keep silent if I have it right," Powder said. And after a moment of quiet he added, "I've been worrying about that."

Fleetwood shook her head and said, "You have a capacity for churning up my insides in about two seconds flat."

"We'll all have plenty of time to relax when we're dead," Powder said.

Fleetwood emptied her drink on his head.

Slowly he raised his eyes.

She said, "You don't know how much better I feel now."

Powder rubbed his face and started to laugh.

Fleetwood sat looking smug.

Powder stood up. "Come on," he said. "Let's go for a walk since you hate dancing so much."

They circumnavigated Lockerbie Square and were silent for several minutes.

As they started around again Powder asked about Clive Burrus.

"I talked to one of his friends. And to him for about a minute."

"He remember you?"

"Nope. I thought he would, but he didn't."

"It's the face out of context. Drink must have dulled his associative intelligence."

"Oh."

"So what did you get?"

"From his friend, that he is generally a fastidious dresser."

"Is he, now?"

"And couldn't say whether he might have had a live-in girlfriend."

"What does Burrus do for a living?"

"He's in an insurance company's actuarial department."

"Did this friend know you are a cop?"

"Yes."

Powder thought about it. Then he asked, "And what about the private eye type? Find anything out about him?"

"A bit," Fleetwood said quietly.

"Don't play games. Sure, he's my kid. But I want to know what you found out that I don't already know."

"They like him. Sociable. Easygoing."

"I wasn't thinking about a personality reference for sharing a desert island. What's he up to?"

Fleetwood said, "He seems to be doing well, and the prosperity is shared by a group of three or four people that he hangs out with."

"Did you get what they were doing?"

"No."

"Why not?"

"Because I didn't."

"What else?"

"He's a couple with the woman of the house."

"For long?"

"I had the feeling it was a couple of months."

"And how long has the 'prosperity' been going?"

"Not long either."

"Names of the others?"

Fleetwood hesitated. "If you get on to something, will you turn it over to—"

"To the detectives? How could I do that? I got no body to make them get out of their chairs for."

"There is a social group. I don't know that everyone is involved in the business activities."

"Grove, Hurst, Mrs. Lee I know," Powder said. "Any others?"

Fleetwood gave him two other names.

Powder repeated them. Then he turned his nose to the sky and said, "What a lovely night."

"Isn't it."

"You have Clive Burrus's home address on the file, don't you?"

"Yes," Fleetwood said.

"I'm tired. You ready to take me home?"

"All right."

He turned to her. "Hey, you know what?"

"What?"

"In the whole party, nobody guessed my costume. What do you think of that?"

"What is it? Mental cripple?"

"Now, that's not nice," Powder said, smiling.

"So what's your costume?"

"Sure you don't know?"

"No."

"I thought sure *you'd* guess it."

She was silent.

"I'm dressed as a troglodyte," he announced with a flourish. "Come on. You knew all the time, didn't you?"

22

*R*icky did not appear for breakfast. Powder ate quickly and then left home for his garden.

But contrary to his Saturday routine, he did not work there. He picked some fruit, put it in a bag, and drove to County Hospital.

The nurse in charge on Jane Doe's ward told Powder that the hospital psychiatrist was with the patient.

Powder used the time to telephone Detective Division, which he routinely did on weekends. He asked for messages.

There was nothing from Bull, but Mrs. Woods had asked him to call.

He called Mrs. Woods.

"My sister here. You want to go to hospital?"

"I'm at the hospital now," Powder said. "Can you get here or shall I pick you up?"

"We get here."

"I'll be free in about three quarters of an hour."

They agreed on a place to meet.

Aurora Sheila Smith Jane Doe looked surprised to see Powder as he walked in.

"What's the verdict?" he asked. "You sane?"

She said, "That's the question to put to him."

"OK," Powder said, as he sat down. "Then tell me whether he's sane."

The woman smiled momentarily, then dropped her eyes.

"It's one of my days off," Powder said. "I tell you that so you will be disarmed and treat this as a social call and tell me all your secrets. Do you like cherries?"

He thrust the bag of fruit he carried onto the bed beside her and pulled up a chair. "Fresh picked today. I grow them myself. Got a little plot on the edge of town that I've been working on for a few years. It keeps me from killing myself when I get low. Go on. Try some."

Slowly the woman opened the bag and took out some cherries.

"I've been thinking about you," Powder said.

"Oh yes?"

"How's your face?"

Some of the bandages were off, and the woman felt the others. "It's all right."

"Good. Yes, I've been thinking that it's about time you told me about yourself."

"You said that the last time you came here."

"No, I didn't," Powder said. "I said it was time you told me who you are, your name, that kind of thing. This is different."

"Is it?"

"Sure. You can tell me about your problem in a hypothetical way. You know, like 'I've got a friend in thus and so situation.' Then I'll nod and say, 'My oh my, has she thought of this,' and you'll say, 'Damn me, no, she hasn't,' and then things will be better. How's that grab you? You can tell I'm an all-right guy, one you can trust, because I brought you a bag of fruit that I grew myself. On an off day. How's the cherries?"

The woman said, "Nice."

"So, don't tell me about yourself. Tell me about your friend."

The woman spent a long time taking pits out of her mouth. She put them in an ashtray beside the bed before she said, "I wouldn't know where to begin."

"The usual thing is to begin at the beginning. But because I'm a right guy who brings you fruit, you can begin anywhere. Any one fact."

"It's hard."

"Be real careful. Cage it all so that I won't be able to figure out who your friend is, but so I'll understand better why she got herself into what she got herself into."

"Innocence," the woman said.

Powder felt that he had finally broken through.

"What kind of innocence?" he asked easily.

"I never really believed that people were *bad*," she said, and then she closed her eyes, and breathed heavily and suffered before him.

She said, "Everybody always said there were bad ones, but I thought it was just the easy way out. The people I knew when I grew up were so basically good. Giving up time, helping . . ."

She was quiet. Powder finally asked, "Do you want me to ask questions?"

"My friend," she said suddenly, "was in a position of trust, and she betrayed it."

"Was this money trust?"

"No, no, no, no. Human trust. Dealing with . . ." she hesitated, thoughtfully. "With people."

"I see," Powder said quietly.

Tears began to well in the woman's eyes, but then subsided. "There was this, this man."

Powder nodded gently.

"He raped me in, in a store closet."

Powder looked on, his face hard.

The woman said simply, "And that was neither here nor there. Oh, it was awful, and wrong, and vile, and hurt, but when it was over, it was a fact and wasn't important, in itself. But he was so, so grief stricken. He fell on his knees. And he cried and he said he was sorry and he asked me to forgive him."

"And?"

"So, of course I forgave him." She shrugged, as if it had all been done lightly. "I knew a lot about forgiveness from the other side. It was a chance to pass some on."

The woman sighed short quick breaths. She laughed momentarily. "I didn't realize that people could be *bad*. Not real people." She brought herself back, took a deeper breath, and looked around. "So it was all right for a while, but then he came to my apartment one afternoon for some help."

"And you let him in?"

"He needed help," she said as if that explained all. "I can see I don't have to tell you, it happened again. And," she said, again mock-lightly, "it was then I found out about evil. Because," she said, "because after it was over he wasn't sorry at all. He said that he would return from time to time and that there was nothing I could do about it, because I hadn't reported him in the first place and now that it had happened again, if I brought in the police, then it would all fall back on me and not on him."

"And you accepted that that was the situation?" Powder said, almost unable to keep his voice colorless.

"Not altogether. But I was in this position of trust, and there were other factors." She tossed her head back and said quickly, "It was hard for me to become what I was. It took . . . a long time, and people helped me. I . . . I am an only child and my . . . parents have clear ideas about what is right." She laughed. "And I didn't realize yet how bad bad can be."

"It already sounds pretty bad to me," Powder said, being sympathetic.

"Oh, it's easy for you," the woman snapped. "You come across murderers and wickedness all the time. But I wasn't raised that way. I lived in a protected environment. I didn't even watch the news on television very often, because it was so horrible. Hilarious, yes?"

"What did you do?" Powder asked.

"After he left? I got up," she said with an awkward smirk on her face. "I dusted myself off. I went out with my boyfriend. Oh yes, I had a boyfriend then. One I even let make love to me sometimes. I'm a goody-goody, but I'm the modern kind of goody-goody, you see." Suddenly she snapped her head from left to right to left to right.

When she spoke again she sounded bitter. "But this, my dear Lieutenant, isn't helping you understand why I did what I did. So let me put you out of your misery while I wallow in mine. The first thing was that I saw people, some people, some people who knew the . . . man. I saw them look at me differently after a week or two. During which time, I may say, he didn't come back. But then he did, and I wouldn't let him in, but he threatened he would tell some of those I couldn't let be told. And another time he even tricked his way in, saying he had a telegram." She gave a chuckle. "You see how gullible? And he demanded a key, and took one and I had the locks changed, and he stole my key. And he drove me away in my own car once. And so on and so on and so on, until I was not a shadow of my former glorious self."

She took a bow and then on her own initiative became subdued again. She said, "My boyfriend and I agreed to a parting of the ways, because I had gone strange and wouldn't answer serious questions seriously."

"How long did this go on?"

"We are talking about the passage of eleven weeks in the life of . . . yours truly."

Powder didn't speak.

Quietly she said, "In fact, I found myself beginning to think about killing him." She uttered a brief sound of disbelief. "Isn't that amazing! Someone like me, who would never conceive how these people I would sometimes read about could plot murder. Yet it happened. I planned it, and thought about it. I got to the point of setting dates and times and places. And I bought the gun."

"And?"

"And then he went and got himself killed doing something else."

"The man was killed?" Powder asked.

"Shot dead. Ironic, yes?"

"Nothing to do with you?"

"Nothing whatsoever."

Powder was silent.

She said, expansively, "When I heard that, I couldn't believe it. And when I believed it, I felt so much joy and pleasure . . ." She sighed. Then became hard. "I felt so much ecstasy in the news of his death, that I felt that I didn't deserve to live. I was capable of cold-blooded murder. I knew that *I* was bad. And not fit to live."

Powder waited again, but this time she seemed content to speak no more. So Powder said, "And that's why?"

"And that's why," she said. She began to laugh. Then cried. Powder listened.

He helped himself to some cherries and offered her some.

She took one.

He asked, "Why the way you did it?"

"My parents shouldn't know. They're old. I adopted them when they were already nearly in their fifties and I've already caused them troubles, in my day. They don't know anything about this kind of world. Better for me to vanish. Just disappear. Which, my dear Lieutenant, is what I would like you to do just now."

Powder thought for a moment. He rose and left.

23

*P*owder waited twenty minutes at the hospital entrance closest to the morgue. He felt numb and insufficient after his interview with Jane Doe. Neither feeling was one he had much experience with. From the time he saw Mrs. Woods and her sister, Mrs. Gilkis sobbed.

"Sorry," Mrs. Woods said to Powder. "Like this since morning. No stop."

Nor did the sobbing stop in the morgue. The distraught mother could not be made to take more than a glance at the body of the woman who might be her child. No answers to the necessary questions were extractable.

"I always sensible one," Mrs. Woods said as she and Powder led Mrs. Gilkis back up to the ground floor.

"I don't know what to say to you," Powder said tiredly. "It's not going to get sorted out until someone who knows your niece makes an accurate decision about that body."

"I give her day. If no, then try bring husband."

Powder acceded to Mrs. Woods's judgment without comment.

Mrs. Woods, however, commented. "Leon going to beat. Strict man."

* * *

Powder drove from the hospital to Northwestern Avenue, a few blocks south of Thirty-eighth Street. There he rang the bell of a substantial brick house set back from the road in sheltered grounds of perhaps three quarters of an acre. After nearly a minute, a short blond woman, carefully turned out, opened the door.

"Is Agnes here, please?" Powder asked.

"I don't know," the woman said with finality and a distinctly British accent. "Who are you?"

Powder told her his name.

"Am I supposed to know you?"

"I don't know. Are you related to Agnes?"

"Only her bloody mother."

"Agnes works mornings for me."

"She said she worked for the police," the woman said, expressing slight distaste.

"Yes."

"So you're the police. You want to do me a favor?"

"What would that be, Mrs. Shorter?"

"Fire the kid. Give her the old heave-ho."

"Why would that be a favor?"

"Because that damn job pays for her bloody computer course and I am so goddamned sick and tired of bloody computers morning, noon, and night that I could scream. In fact, I think I will."

The woman screamed.

When she had finished, she said, "I just long for the days when a chip was greasy and fried and made of potato instead of micro. Oh, bloody hell. It's not your fault my husband and my daughter talk in riddles, is it? You want to know if the young genius is here. I suppose I should find out for you. In fact, I think I will."

Powder waited on the doorstep.

In less than a minute the woman returned to say, "The news is that she has gone to work."

"Work?" Powder asked. "The office is closed over the weekend. Would that mean to school?"

"No," the woman said definitely. "My husband and daughter are fussy about that kind of thing. If the word is 'work,' then 'work' is the word."

"All right. Thank you."

"Mr. Powder, may I ask whether you know how to program a computer?"

"I can read what's printed on the monitor screen if it's in English," Powder said.

"What a relief. I'd like to shake your hand on that. In fact, I think I will."

Agnes was, indeed, working at the computer terminal in the Missing Persons office. Powder entered and stood behind her as she punched and frowned and wrote and punched some more.

"What the hell are you doing here, Agnes?"

Speaking her words between tapping phrases on the keyboard, she said, "It's . . . easier to get . . . stretches of . . . time on the main computer . . . weekends."

Powder went to the telephone on his desk.

He called the campsite manager of McCormick's Creek State Park.

"I've been wondering about this fellow Weaver," Powder said.

"He's here," the man said. "That's the most I can say about him."

"What do you mean?"

"I mean he's here. He's set up his tent and he's stayed in it."

"All the time?"

"All the time."

"Alone?"

"Alone. Far as I can tell. If a fella doesn't go out, kind

of makes it hard to poke around, you know what I mean?"

After hanging up, Powder restlessly returned to his place standing behind Agnes, who, finally, leaned back and said, "They're awkward in Hammond, but I've got them."

"That's a fine piece of work. Fine," Powder said. "I'd like to pat you on the back for that. In fact, I think I will." He thumped her on the back. "So, what the hell are you talking about?"

"I've been working on your travel-nap problem," Agnes said.

"And?"

"I've got some more positives. All in the last three years, and totaling seven with the three incidents we got from our own computers."

"Summarize."

"The four new cases are all women. Two are actual naps with no further information on the fate of the victims. The third was taken and the body recovered two weeks later, in the country. Physical and sexual abuse. Other one was an attempt which did not succeed."

Powder rubbed his face with both hands. "Ages?"

"Twenty to fifty. All traveling alone. Altogether three buses, three planes, one train."

Powder said, "The one whose body was found. Not burned by any chance?"

"Nothing like that on the primary entry," Agnes said.

Powder thought again. "What about dates?"

"Nothing too clear. But one of the attempts was followed within three days by one of the successes. And if you list the others it would be arguable that the intervals are quantum defined."

"What the hell does that mean?"

Agnes showed Powder the complete list of incidents and dates on the terminal screen. "Look. There and there the gap is about three months between naps."

"Yes?"

"And there and there it is about six months and there about nine months."

"Eight and a bit," Powder said, but he nodded.

"The intervals are in quanta of three months," Agnes said. "It may be a coincidence. But if not, it could mean that there are other incidents we don't know about yet which would fit in the spaces. Or it could tell you something about who is doing it, if they're all being done by the same person."

"Where have they taken place?"

"The three here. One each in Fort Wayne, South Bend, Lafayette, and Bloomington."

Powder rubbed his face. "All Indiana, huh?"

Severely, Agnes said, "The state computers are the only ones I have demand access to. But get into Chicago or Louisville or Cincinnati and you may fill in those three-month spots."

"All a bit scattered, here and there," Powder said reflectively.

Agnes shrugged.

"Put it all together. Words of two syllables, so the Homicide people can understand it. And stick Marianna Gilkis at the bottom saying Sergeant Bull already has details on her. Mark it extremely urgent. Then take it upstairs."

"OK, Lieutenant." Agnes beamed.

"Since you're already here," he said, "there's something else I want you to do."

"What's that, Lieutenant?"

"I want to know about men who have been shot recently."

"Shot," Agnes repeated.

"Probably in the last couple of weeks, but call it four.

And probably in the course of some crime, but make it any man shot and killed."

"In Indianapolis?"

"And environs. Whatever they've got on file."

Agnes nodded.

"I met your mother today."

"Oh?"

"She doesn't seem wholly entranced by your preoccupation with microtechnology."

"She thinks there's something wrong with a girl who would rather curl up on a couch with a program than some octopus of a boy," Agnes said dismissively. "Anyway, I've got a boyfriend. We make up video games together." She turned back to the machine.

Feeling at least a generation out of touch, Powder left the office.

He drove along West Washington Street and took the last left before crossing Eagle Creek. He pulled up in front of a former lumberyard bounded by tall, barb-topped link fences.

A free-swinging sign that hung out from the main building advertised the services of a private investigator, Albert Samson.

The venetian blinds in the broad front window were closed, but Powder went to the door as if he expected it to be unlocked. Which it was.

Inside, a stocky man in his forties was leaning back in a swivel chair, tapping the keys of an electric typewriter with his toes.

Powder stood in the doorway, but the show stopped abruptly as Samson realized someone was there.

"Mr. Lieutenant Leroy Powder, M.A., College of Life," Samson said. "As I live and breathe."

"I wasn't sure you were still in business. Are you?" Powder asked coldly.

"Thriving. I even have to set Saturday mornings aside for paperwork."

"I suppose," Powder said, gesturing to an upright piano in the corner, "that you play that with your nose."

"You'd be surprised," Samson said. Then thought. "Perhaps not. Have you lost weight? Let me get you a beer."

"Never drink the stuff," Powder said.

Samson got two beers.

"What can I do for you, Leroy?"

"Some routine surveillance work."

Samson blinked. Then he pinched himself. "You mean," he asked slowly, doubtfully, "surveillance *work*? For payment?"

"Do you like fresh vegetables and fruit?" Powder asked.

In the late afternoon, Powder returned to police headquarters. He went first to Homicide to ask what had happened since Agnes's report was sent up.

He was told that it had been read, then put in Bull's pigeonhole because it referred to one of his cases. It was still there. Bull wasn't around.

Powder blew his top. He spelled the word "urgent" for them. He defined it from a dictionary. He screamed.

Bull was called.

Powder went downstairs to the Missing Persons office. There he found a small stack of incident-summary printout sheets. All dealt with recently shot men. Though he had intended to read them on the spot, he was too angry. He packed up the reports and took them home.

24

While Powder was reading the Sunday paper, Ricky came home. It was quarter to eleven.

Powder said, "You look exhausted."

"I am. I'm going to bed."

"Real live wire, is she?" Powder asked, and he winked exaggeratedly.

Ricky began to say one thing but then said, "Yeah, wild," instead.

"I don't know how you youngsters keep it up," Powder said pointedly. "And after a groovy party night on Friday too. I suppose you're off and at it again when the chimes strike for noon. You're something else, Richard, you really are."

Ricky passed his father, went into his bedroom and closed the door.

Powder telephoned the site manager at McCormick's Creek.

"That Weaver guy, he's gone," the man said.

"Has he indeed," Powder said.

"Pulled out half an hour ago. I saw his car go by, all filled up."

"You haven't been to his site, have you?"

"I have. I have," the man said, rather proudly. "Went there right off."

"And?"

"And nothing."

"It is exactly as it was before?"

"Bit clearer, if anything."

"No other signs of disturbance? Nothing left behind? Nothing in the grass?"

"Didn't have much in the way of grass to start. Sorry not to be more of a help."

Powder called Carollee Fleetwood.

"How are you at making picnic lunches?" Powder asked.

"What the hell are you on about this time, Powder?"

"Not so good, huh? That's all right. I'll bring the food. Pick you up in about an hour," he said.

"I think we'll go in my car," Powder said when Fleetwood answered her door. "Hurry up. There are some things I want to talk to you about."

Fleetwood's face advertised internal conflict.

He laughed at her. "If you tell me to get stuffed, you'll miss the action. Come on. Get your Frisbee and let's go."

"Is this work or play, Powder?" she asked sternly.

"The only way I know how to live," he said suddenly, "is to combine the two. My ex-wife used to say it meant I was going to die young, but she got tired of waiting. Now, are you going to get together whatever you need or do you have to do another ten minutes' falling off your crutches before we leave?"

He wasn't quite sure how to begin as he set about lifting her out of her chair.

"No need to be fussy," she said.

Gently he eased his arms under her, lifted, and placed her in the passenger seat of his car.

Perspiration stood out suddenly on his brow.

"What's the heat for, Powder? Am I that heavy or is it the thrill of the touch?"

"Just as well you can't tell," Powder said defensively.

"Who says?" she said. "And is that a clean shirt? Jesus, you smell like sweaty laundry."

They drove out Kentucky Avenue and Route 67, the highway to Spencer. The town was about fifty miles away. Powder talked about Aurora Jane Doe.

Fleetwood said, "You did well."

"I thought so too until I got the list of gunshot killings from Agnes."

"And?"

"In the last four weeks nobody in town has been shot dead who could remotely be described as having a job where there are 'positions of trust.' We got two chronic unemployeds in domestic situations, two druggies—one of whom was a school kid—both in the course of robberies, and a pro burglar who was surprised, got shot, and went over a fourth-floor ledge and broke his back. There were various nonfatal shooting incidents, but I wonder whether she was making the whole damn thing up."

"Do you think she was?"

"No," Powder said. "I believe every word."

In Spencer, which claimed fame as the childhood home of the mother of British Prime Minister Harold Macmillan, they turned left on Indiana 46 and three miles later arrived at McCormick's Creek State Park.

The campsite manager introduced himself as Ramey Fry, and grew visibly excited when Powder told him who he was.

"You come all the way down here? Must be something important, huh, mister?"

"We were just out for a ride and a picnic," Powder said. "Show the man our basket, Carollee, honey."

Fleetwood sat sternly.

"And since we were in the vicinity, I thought we might as well stop here as anyplace, since you'd been so helpful."

"But you're a policeman?"

"That's right."

Fry clucked. "Whatever you say, mister. But you want to see the site the guy used, don't you?"

Powder looked back at Fleetwood and appeared to think. "Well, I suppose we might as well. What you think, Carollee, honey?"

The campsite was as isolated as Fry had said it was on the telephone.

When they got to it, Powder parked behind Fry's pickup and unloaded Fleetwood into her chair. He pushed her down the gentle slope to the level that Fry identified for them. "This here is it," Fry said.

Powder rubbed his face. The area was bare of grass in an oval larger than any likely tent. The soil was pretty level, lightly gritted, but with little in the way of surface rock. It was patchily streaked with lighter-colored, lighter-textured material. Powder walked across it, springing slightly on the soles of his feet as if testing it.

Then he walked a loop around the edge of the area until he had found four or five places where there were small holes.

"These look like where tent pegs were to you?" Powder asked.

"Oh yeah," Fry said easily.

Powder scuffed marks with his heel connecting the peg

holes and he quickly had an outline of the approximate area that Weaver's tent had covered.

To Fleetwood he said, "Inside my pretty picture, does the ground look completely level to you?"

Fleetwood looked. "Not *completely,*" she said. "But just about."

"Does it look like it goes up, or goes down, where it's not flat?"

"Up a little. There," she said, pointing to a slight rise toward the back of the area.

Powder went to Fry, who had watched the process patiently. "Mr. Fry, Carollee and I seem to think that the ground rises a little bit inside my circle. What do you think?"

Fry, unable to work up enthusiasm for a subject that seemed so undramatic, said, "Yeah. I guess."

"I suppose you don't recall whether it was like that before?"

Fry shrugged.

"I tell you what I really want," Powder said easily, fixing the man's eyes.

"What's that now?"

"I would like to find out what's underneath that little rise."

"Underneath it?" Fry scratched the back of his head. "You mean, like, underneath?"

"That's right," Powder said. "Kind of unofficial, you know? But if you could find me a couple of guys willing to do some digging there, well, I'd pay them for their time and trouble and that would include filling it back in after, and the rent for the site as well. Do you think you could arrange that for me, Mr. Fry?"

"Plain yogurt, lettuce, unsalted peanuts, oranges." Powder rooted exaggeratedly through the box of food he'd brought. "Don't make a face. I invited you to do the catering."

"Are you going to tell me about it?"

"Just—I don't know—not a hunch exactly. But the conclusion of the logic of the situation."

"We're talking about William G. Weaver, Junior, I take it?"

"Yes," Powder said. He leaned back on the grass and looked up Fleetwood's skirt. "I have a confession to make," he said.

"What?"

"I *am* suspicious of Weaver. I can't bear it. That calm. I've met a few self-contained people on this job in my time, but he's so colorless that it has to be phony. Has to."

"You're getting emotional all of a sudden," Fleetwood said. "At least for a frosty, controlled son of a bitch."

"Me? Controlled?" Powder protested. He found a seed stem of some long grass, and chewed the end.

"It's all plot and posture, I suppose," Fleetwood said.

Powder shrugged by wagging his grass.

He said, "So Weaver goes through the motions. Reports her missing, calls her relatives. All that. But then he comes camping alone and never goes out of his tent. He could do that in his backyard. Why here?"

"OK. Why here?"

"I say he killed his wife. I say he stored her body till this trip. I say he stayed in the tent because he was burying her."

"What else could make sense?" Fleetwood asked easily. "So you've come down to dig her up."

"Yeah," Powder said. "Want some herb tea?"

They ate near a little waterfall in the creek canyon, and after they finished, Powder pushed Fleetwood leisurely back to the campsite, some two miles.

Ramey Fry saw them coming and met them fifty yards from the hole. "I was about to come and get you," he said.

"Why's that?" Powder asked.

"We dug out the bit you wanted, and got down about two and a half, three feet."

"Yeah?"

"And we hit solid rock. Kind of a layer, just after we were through the subsoil. So what you want us to do?"

Powder pushed Fleetwood to the edge of the hole in silence. A mass of earth was piled alongside and a squat, well-muscled boy with no shirt smiled up as Powder looked down. The boy clanked his shovel on several spots at the bottom of the hole.

"It's all around, mister," the boy said.

Powder rubbed his face. He looked at his watch, and pulled out his wallet.

"It wasn't hard digging, mister," the boy said, intending to make Powder feel better.

25

*I*t wasn't until they picked up the divided highway outside of Martinsville that the silence in the car was broken.

"Come off it, Powder," Fleetwood said. "You can't be right all the time."

Holding the steering wheel with his knees, Powder rubbed his face with both hands.

Fleetwood waited, but he said nothing.

"Stop being a baby," she said.

"I wasn't thinking about that."

"Your black hole?"

"No."

"What? Sulking because you didn't get a straight story out of Jane Doe?"

"No, that neither," he said.

"Well, why are you looking so miserable? Punishing yourself for being relaxed and almost human for a while this afternoon?"

"I was just thinking that I will probably have my son arrested before long."

Fleetwood was stopped.

"He's spending more money than he's earning and I figure the least he's doing is bugging jobs by himself for a private detective agency and evading taxes. But I'm worried about this stuff with his friends. He may be looking at jail time instead of a fine or suspended sentence."

"How sure are you?"

"I could be surer."

"Oh," Fleetwood said.

"I warned him to stop." Powder shrugged. "What else is available to a good cop?"

Fleetwood was quiet for a moment while she worked out that Powder assumed his warning would go unheeded.

"You're full of surprises, Powder," she said.

"Hell, I may be wrong. It isn't the day for me to claim infallibility."

"Tell me something else."

"What?"

"Who's going to pay for your hole?"

He looked at her.

"That means you, I take it."

"I only claim back when I'm right. Doesn't do to let the bastards know about my mistakes. Not when they're nearly as eager to get rid of me as they are to get rid of you."

"So, we were off duty today?"

"Yeah."

"OK. Just wanted to know."

He said, "If you want to claim time back for this little fiasco, that's all right."

They rode to the city limits in silence.

Suddenly Powder said, "Do you like beans? Fresh beans?"

After a moment, Fleetwood said, "Yes."

He took her to his garden. Carefully settling her in the wheelchair he said, "I'm getting better at this."

"I can only tell by looking for bruises."

"The beans are over there," he said. "Go pick some."

He left her on the uneven ground at the edge of his parking space and went to one of his sheds, where he got out a hoe.

Fleetwood made her way to the beans. Powder hoed furiously.

After twenty minutes he stopped, returned to the shed, and traded the hoe for a plastic bag. He brought the bag, and a towel, to the beans.

"Firsts on the towel?"

Fleetwood took it and mopped her brow. Powder bagged the beans she had picked.

As she handed the towel back to him she said, "Take me home, will you, Lieutenant?"

He wheeled her back to the car.

He took her to the door of her house. She said, "I got a little bit tired out there."

"On warm days, it holds the heat," he said. "Because it's in a hollow. I have a lot of trouble with fungus diseases."

She opened the door.

"OK," he said. "Here's your beans."

She turned her head to him. "Are you leaving?" she asked sharply.

He faced her without speaking.

"Either come in and make love to me or take your goddamn beans with you." She threw the bag on the walk and banged the door with a fist as she went into the house.

Powder took a shower and then washed her down.

"Any bruises?" she asked.

Later she said, "You know the only reason you're here?"

"No."

"Ever since I knew I was going to work for you, I've

been hearing about this bragging that you only have seven toes."

He said nothing.

She looked up at him. "Well, there have been quite a few guys wanting to be where you are now."

Powder stayed where he was.

"But I decided to save myself for another cripple."

Powder gave her something. He said, "I got them caught in a trapdoor when I was a kid." Then, "Look, you want those beans or not?"

"Don't tell me you cook too?"

"No. But you do, don't you?"

26

On Monday morning Powder got up early, ate, and was waiting in Detective Division when Bull arrived.

But the young sergeant stole the initiative by saying, "Got my message, then?"

"What message?"

"About the decision on the file your kid sent up."

"What decision?"

"We're holding a meeting on it this morning, at eleven."

"It was on your desk two days ago," Powder said pointedly.

"You want to come or not? I told them you should come."

"Damn right I'll come."

"And another thing," Bull said.

Powder looked skeptical.

"Wasn't there something on report from you the other day about television and video sets?"

"Yes," Powder said slowly.

"Well, you remember that taxi driver?"

Powder was silent.

"Well, I eliminated him from the burned body because the company records showed he was working regularly all that night except for coffee stops. He came down and we went through his sheet. And the other drivers confirm he was with them at the usual times and wasn't acting strangely."

"So?"

"They also say he's been offering secondhand video sets around, cheap. Thought you might want his address."

When Powder came back to the office, Fleetwood said, "Good morning."

He glared at her. He said, "Don't just sit there. Go out and do something."

"Like what?"

"I'll give you a choice of two."

"Why do I have this feeling I'm not going to like it?"

"You don't like choice? You can do them both."

"Thanks."

"Number one. Go out and see an ex-taxi driver about some television sets. Number two. Go to the hospital and have a little talk with Jane Doe."

"About what?"

"Tell her that the 'man' giving her trouble was a sixteen-year-old boy called Harold Sillit and that the responsible job she had was as a high school teacher. See what she has to say about that."

The meeting at eleven turned out to be an affair of six officers: Captain Gartland, two lieutenants from outside sections—one of whom was Tidmarsh, the computer supremo—two sergeants including Bull. And Powder.

Gartland opened proceedings in a surprisingly personal way. "You've all heard of Powder, even if you haven't run into him. Most of what you've heard is probably bad. Troublemaking, time wasting, clogging up the works. But sometimes the guy comes up with the goods, which is why he wasn't out on his duff a long time ago. What we're trying to decide here is whether this is one of those times."

Powder sat stonefaced while the others rattled copies of Agnes's report.

"In his zeal to stick a name on a corpse that Sergeant Bull here is responsible for, Powder had his secretary—"

Powder interrupted to correct, "My computer operative."

"Shut up," Gartland said. "Powder had his goddamn secretary absorbing all available general computer time. The justification is a suggestion that there is a pattern to, maybe even a link between, a statewide series of serious offenses. You've had copies of the report. What I want to decide this morning is whether there is enough here to indicate if there might really be a connection between these incidents and if so, what we should do next."

Powder was back in the office at ten to twelve. He said to Agnes, "Been nice to know you, kid."

"Lieutenant?"

"You're being kicked upstairs."

"What?"

"To act as secretary to a team that's following up your travel-kidnap report."

"Yeah?"

"You get to try to fill in the holes, working in the computer section with Lieutenant Tidmarsh."

"Yeah?" Her reaction was pleasurable anticipation.

"All sounds a little farfetched to me. But you're to report upstairs to Captain Gartland."

"Is this to be a permanent reassignment?"

"Not yet. But once Tidmarsh gets over the disappointment of your not being Fleetwood, it'll be a chance for you, kid. If you want it. So pull your plug out and get the hell upstairs."

Powder called Mrs. Woods when Agnes had gone.

"I call police yesterday. You out," she said.

"A day off, Mrs. Woods."

"Oh."

"I was calling about your brother-in-law. What did you call me about?"

"The same. He no come."

"I don't understand," Powder said.

"He no come. He after John Langston."

"Who is John Langston?"

"He reason Marianna sent here."

Powder rubbed his face with his free hand, thinking suddenly that he had never asked Mrs. Woods why her niece, who knew nobody in Indianapolis, should abruptly remove herself to live with an aunt who didn't know her well enough to identify her body.

"Tell me about it."

"John Langston no-good boyfriend. Leon send Marianna to me. Now Marianna disappear. Leon say he kill when he catch them. He say no point coming. Body not Marianna."

"How is your sister, Mrs. Woods?"

"Something better."

"If she could look at the corpse again and give us a decision, it would help a great deal."

"It hard."

"Things are going to get complicated if we don't have an identification. It might end up with the police making your brother-in-law come here."

"Make Leon terrible mad."

"Could that possibility help your sister face the ordeal?"

"Maybe," Mrs. Woods said.

"I'll ask the hospital to look out for you and help you as much as they can."

Fleetwood returned to the office at a few minutes after twelve. It was much too early for her to be back.

"Number one," she said, "your television taxi man was not at home. At least that's what his landlady said. And he lives on the second floor. I can't do second floors yet."

Powder sat.

"Number two," she said. "Jane Doe ducked out of the hospital this morning."

"The hell she did," he said quietly.

"I tried to get more information, but there isn't a lot. A nurse found the bed empty about seven. No one around the place spotted her leaving."

Powder thought. He said, "It feels wrong."

"What do you mean?"

"Phooey," he said. "Suddenly this has become one of those days."

"You get yourself personally involved in all these cases," she said.

"Is that supposed to be a newsflash?" he snapped.

A boy of about sixteen entered the office and stood uneasily just inside the doorway.

Powder saw him and took a deep breath. "Can I help you?"

"Hope so," the boy drawled. "My brother been gone a week and our folks don't make no never mind."

The telephone rang.

Powder answered the telephone. Fleetwood saw to the young man.

The phone call was from Major Tafelski, his Monday inquiry about developments in the case of his missing sister.

Powder reported none, hung up, and sat at his desk, head in hands, for several minutes, as Fleetwood dealt with the boy's concern.

"Don't sit like that," Fleetwood said, when the boy left. "Gives the section a bad image."

"I think . . ." Powder said slowly, "that I am losing my grip. Nothing feels right or sane or settled anymore."

Fleetwood raised her eyebrows.

"I want you to go out," Powder said.

"Again?"

Powder wrote a name and address. "Question the major about his missing sister. Put a little pressure on him."

"Can I eat first?"

"No. I want you to go there now."

"What's the urgency?"

"Just do it, will you?" He looked up at her. He almost said, "Please?"

She went.

Powder sat again at his desk, his hands over his eyes.

He shook himself. He called Detective Division to find out who had handled the death of Harold Sillit twelve days before. It was on the file of a Detective Sergeant Brindell.

Powder called Brindell and raised the name of the case.

"I remember vaguely," Brindell said. "Kid killed sticking up a late-night fruit stand? Nothing to it. That the one you mean?"

"He was sixteen, right?"

"If you say so."

"It says so on the print-out. What I wanted to know was what school he went to."

"School? A stickup kid. Woulda dropped out, wouldn't he?"

"I have reason to believe he was in school. Don't you know?"

"It was all a formality."

"So you don't know."

"And I don't care," Brindell said.

Powder took the boy's address and found it on a map of Indianapolis. Geographically, it seemed likely that his school would have been William Henry Harrison High.

Despite its being summer vacation Powder called Harrison High School.

There was no answer.

Powder called the board of education and got the names and home numbers of the principal and assistant principal.

Eventually, from the assistant principal, Powder learned that a social studies teacher of Jane Doe's general description had quit suddenly, two weeks before.

"Any explanation?" Powder asked.

"None," the woman said. "She sent a letter. It said, 'I am forced by circumstances to give up this post.' "

"Was she having problems?"

"No," the assistant principal said thoughtfully. "Maybe some discipline trouble, but nothing unusual for a first-year teacher."

"This was her first year?"

"Yes."

"Is it common for someone to quit like this?"

"No. If they were disillusioned with teaching, perhaps. But Miss Crismore was, well, outspokenly idealistic."

"This is faculty lounge reputation?"

"That's right."

"Do you remember what college she came from?"

"I think it was Hanover College."

"Near Madison?"

"Yes."

"And do you know where she came from originally?"

"I don't know that."

"Would it be possible for you to find out for me?"

The assistant principal said, "It might be on an employment card in the school. Lieutenant, is Sarah Crismore in some kind of trouble?"

"I explained that I am with the missing persons section," Powder said. "It's possible she can help us."

"But why are you asking for her original home address instead of her current address?"

"I was getting to that," he said. "Do you know her address here?"

"No," the assistant principal said.

"But maybe you could find that out for me too?"

"If it's important."

Powder continued, oblivious to the fishing the assistant principal was doing. "One other thing. I gather she had a gentleman friend at the school."

Silence greeted this bit of guesswork.

"I would appreciate his name," Powder said.

"I have no firsthand knowledge of any special friendships Miss Crismore may have made."

Powder sighed. "He's married, huh? Well, I don't give a damn about that. But I need the man's name. And address. With the other information you are getting for me."

"All right, Lieutenant."

"Good," Powder said chattily. "Not a very good time for the school, is it?"

"What do you mean?"

"I understand you had a bit of trouble lately."

"Trouble?"

"One of your students. Getting killed in a robbery? That was Harrison High, wasn't it? Didn't I read that?"

"Perhaps you also read," the assistant principal said, "the list of our graduating class and of our record number of college placements?"

"Ah. Must have missed that."

"Pity."

"Be hearing from you soon, then."

Powder exhaled heavily as he hung up the telephone. He was oppressively aware of loose ends, in his work and his life.

But instead of thinking, he began to work on the routine updates of the section's outstanding cases.

27

*T*he first reporter to get to Powder was Ben Brown, from the *Star.* "You can't kick me out this time," he said.

"What you want, Ben?"

"Comment, of course. What you think of her, what she has added to the office since she joined your staff last week. That kind of thing."

Powder stared at the man. There was a glint in Brown's eye. Powder said, "We've been able to sell off one of the desk chairs."

"May I quote you?"

"No."

"Well?"

"Well, what?"

"Come on, Powder! You can't sit on it. She's here a week and she decides to visit an old guy who has been calling you every week for years and, wham-bam, she turns up the old guy's sister's skeleton in the spare bedroom. I don't want to shit on you, but you could have done that any day for years, only you didn't. She comes along and a week later it cracks open."

"She's a credit to the force," Powder said histrionically. "I knew from the first day that she would go far." Powder coughed artificially. "If her career keeps rolling the way it has till now, she could go all the way."

"Yeah," Brown said slowly.

Powder looked directly into the man's eyes. "You've never had reason to think I told you anything that wasn't absolutely straight."

"I suppose."

"OK," Powder said. "So get out, will you?"

The man left.

Two more reporters called Powder before twenty past four, when Lieutenant Gaulden appeared in the office.

"Welcome, welcome," Powder said. "Come to congratulate us?"

"It's true, then?"

"Something is," Powder said enigmatically.

"We're hearing that goddamn Fleetwood has turned up a years-old murder. It's all around upstairs. That right?"

"Wouldn't want to commit myself as to whether it is murder or not."

Gaulden tightened his lips and exhaled deeply. "In one week on the job, how would she know where to look?"

"How would anybody know where to look for something like that?" Powder snapped.

And behind Gaulden he saw Fleetwood roll in.

Powder continued, "I could have done it any day for years, but I didn't. She comes in here with a new perspective, a fresh mind. So maybe she gets lucky in that this body was waiting around and it needn't have been. But my only worry is that she's too good a cop and you're not going to let me keep her down here, because you think Missing Persons is a lost and found and only needs one guy half-time to push paper. Oh, hang on. There she is now."

Gaulden turned around.

Powder made his way through the counter-top hatchway, saying, "Welcome back, Sergeant. A good bit of work you did there. We've had the press in already. But have they gotten a picture of you?"

Doubtfully, Fleetwood said, "They took pictures at the scene."

"Great," Powder said. "Great." He clapped Gaulden on the back. "A good little advertisement for a flexible, enlightened police force, eh?"

"Congratulations, Sergeant Fleetwood," Gaulden said.

"Thank you."

Gaulden left.

Powder's smile vanished. "Enter, Indianapolis's answer to Sherlock Holmes," he said and he walked back to the counter, where he held the flap up for her.

"I'm not staying. I've got to go up and check the guy in. I just stopped in to tell you about it."

"Thanks a bundle."

"Really, there was no chance before. First the guy went hysterical, then there were patrol cops and the ambulance. And then the reporters."

Powder nodded.

"I tried telling them it was your idea."

"For God's sake don't do that! If you want to stay in this racket, then you have to play all the angles you can."

"Roy—" she began.

" 'Roy'? 'Roy'? What's with this 'Roy,' Sergeant Fleetwood?"

The telephone rang. Powder answered it sharply. "Lieutenant Roy Powder, Missing Persons."

"Bull here, Powder."

Powder waved Fleetwood away. She turned.

"Hello, Bull."

"I hear congratulations are in order. You guys had a good score today."

"All down to my new sergeant, Carollee Fleetwood." He spelled out the last name. "A real mover."

Fleetwood closed the door behind her.

"What I really called about was to tell you that I may have an ID on my body."

"Yeah?"

"Woman named Gilkis identified it as her daughter. One of your cases."

"Pity," Powder said.

"What?"

"I had a different idea for you on that body," Powder said. "But if you're sure . . ."

"Well, funny you should say."

"Why's that?"

"The husband of the woman apparently swears that it is not the daughter."

"Is the father here?"

"No. In St. Paul. But he says the daughter is in St. Paul. Only me, I figure a mother knows her own kid."

"I suppose," Powder said.

"You know these people, don't you?"

"A little."

"Could you go see the mother? See what's what?"

"You're not so sure?"

"I was. But I'm not."

Powder relented. "I can maybe stop on my way home."

"Great."

Powder waited.

"You said you had another idea. What was that?"

"If I was you," Powder said, "I'd take a guy called Clive Burrus to see this body."

"Yeah . . . ?"

"Only do it hard. *Make* him go. Make him think you know he knows all about it. No answers, only questions."

"What's the story?"

"He's on the list. Missing a girlfriend. I don't like the

way he dresses. No consistency. Unless you're already sure about what you got," Powder said. Then he asked, "How's my kid Agnes Shorter going to work out for you guys?"

"Seems all right."

"All right? The kid's a genius. Anybody from down here is good, but Shorter is special and if you guys don't register that, for Christ's sake, send her back to me."

"Yeah, I said she seemed good."

Powder hung up.

He was about to call Mrs. Woods when a distraught young woman ran in.

"It's Alison," she said. "She's gone!"

It was a quarter to six when the four-year-old was found. She had, simply, wandered off while her mother was shopping downtown in the City Market, which happened to be across the street from the police department.

Powder went home. He felt like a change of clothes and while he was there he made a sandwich.

He also looked in Ricky's room. From the doorway it was clear that his son had moved out.

Powder left for Mrs. Woods's.

"Horrible angry," she said to Powder in the front room. He could hear the sister sobbing elsewhere in the house.

"I'm beginning to wish I had the chance of a few words with this Leon," Powder said.

"Big angry man. Always like that. No good, her. I always know."

"And he says Marianna is in St. Paul?"

"Not seen. But seen John Langston. He say looks know-it-all."

Powder rubbed his face. He was attracted by the simplicity of this way to fill in the missing part of what happened to Marianna Gilkis. If she disappeared between bus and taxi, with her baggage, it was far easier to think she left the station area with someone she knew than with a stranger. And if she had been sent away to separate her from this man, then maybe he had driven down, beating the bus, and was waiting for her when she arrived. Ready to drive back to St. Paul to live happily ever after.

"You were with your sister when she looked at the body in County Hospital," Powder said.

"Yes."

"Do you think she was really sure?"

Mrs. Woods shrugged. "I do my best," she said.

Powder looked at the woman, who seemed, for the moment, hewn from the stuff on which stable civilization is built.

"OK," he said. "Thank you."

Powder drove to the home of William G. Weaver, Jr. He went quickly to the front door, to avoid losing his resolve.

He rang the bell several times, without response.

Powder walked to the garage and looked in. Weaver's car was there. Powder walked around the side to the backyard.

Weaver was watering in a pair of newly planted rosebushes.

"Quite an outdoor man," Powder said as he approached.

Weaver turned quickly as he heard the voice, startled. "Oh," he said. "You scared me."

"Guilty conscience, eh?" Powder said. He gestured to the roses. "New stock?"

"Transplanting."

Carefully, Weaver laid his hose on the ground. "What can I do for you, Lieutenant Powder?"

"Heard from Annie?"

"No."

"Thought of some reason she might lie about going out?"

Weaver shook his head.

Powder took a breath, bit the bullet. "I want to apologize to you."

"What for?"

"I've been hounding you about your wife's disappearance," Powder said easily.

"Oh," Weaver said.

"It's just that I've been working on the presumption that you killed her, but last night when I got back from McCormick's Creek, I decided I was wrong."

"Oh," Weaver said.

Powder held his head, as if in distress. "Damn it. It's been your lack of reaction that's been churning my guts all along. Making me think your wife running around getting tickets *was* something you asked her to do."

Powder looked at the man.

"Nope," Powder said. "I don't buy it again. I take the apology back."

He turned and stomped to his car. Angry, uncertain.

He drove to the boarding house that was the listed address of the taxi driver who'd been trying to sell video sets.

The man was in a second-floor room at the front of the house.

He seemed to be thin, about thirty-five, with receding red hair. But Powder didn't have much chance to confirm the impression or talk to him because when Powder identified himself as a policeman, the man opened his room door, showed his gun, and shot Powder twice.

28

"What are you doing here?"

"I was going to ask you the same question," Fleetwood said.

"Who's manning the office?"

"Agnes is there," Fleetwood said.

"Thought she was gobbled up by special-task-force projects."

"You'll have to hurry back and straighten it all out. How do you feel?"

"Groovy," Powder said.

Fleetwood looked around the room.

"Nice as the one you were in?" Powder asked.

"Mine was much better," she said. "How did it happen, then?"

"Knocked on the door. The guy answered shooting. Simple as that. There I was, all alone. No partner to shove in the way."

Fleetwood said, "They say one broke a rib and the other is still in there, near the spine."

"That's more than they've told me," Powder said.

"And if they hadn't been twenty-twos . . ."

"At least I got feeling in seven of my toes."

"You didn't think you were in danger?"

"A guy about a television? Did you think you were in danger when you went to his place and looked up from the bottom of the stairs?"

Fleetwood said, "They say he's skipped."

"Surprise, surprise," Powder said.

A nurse knocked and then entered the room.

"Time to wipe my nose again already?" Powder asked.

"There's a man out here. Says he's your boss and wants to have a word."

"Yeah, sure."

Fleetwood turned to go.

"Hang on."

"Why?"

"Just get out your notebook."

After a moment, a bear of a man in the dress uniform of a deputy chief entered the room.

Powder said, "And finally I was supposed to have a report from the assistant principal of Harrison High School with home details of a couple of their teachers. Check my desk for it. That's enough for now. I'll get the rest to you by phone in an hour."

"Yes, Lieutenant," Fleetwood said. "Good morning, Chief Snyder."

"Not such a good morning, Sergeant Fleetwood. Shocking news about Powder here, isn't it?"

"Yes, sir."

Snyder looked at her. "Going out the front?"

"I intended to, yes."

"Policy to the press is no comment, except from me."

"Yes, sir." Fleetwood left.

"I don't know how many other officials from the department have conveyed their shock and horror at these events, Lieutenant Powder, but believe me, when I heard about it I was disturbed, very disturbed indeed."

"Your disturbance is gratefully received," Powder said.

"And I want you to know that no effort is being spared in bringing the perpetrator of this deed to justice."

"Thank you, Chief."

The man seemed uncertain whether to sit. He decided to stand.

"I'm pleased to see you so alert."

"I've got to be," Powder said.

"Oh?"

"So undermanned at the office," Powder said. "I've got to help out no matter what."

The deputy chief said, "You've been in the force a long time now."

"Longer than you have," Powder said.

"Really?"

"Though it looks as if I am losing my touch when I let myself be taken out by one guy in a situation like this. I have to ask myself if I am still up to the job."

Snyder looked earnestly at the man in the hospital bed. "I'm sorry to hear you talking like that. A man with your experience, record, and . . . enthusiasm would be a sad loss to the department at any time. But to go out in circumstances like this rather than at a time of your own choosing . . . Well, I never like to see that."

"I rate a full pension, and I'm not spending the money I make now. Be a pity not to have the chance to enjoy the fruit and vegetables of my labors."

Half an hour later Powder called the Missing Persons office.

"I am an idiot," he told Fleetwood. "A scatterbrained idiot. There's no two ways about it, I'm losing my grip."

"What do you want, Lieutenant?"

"Nothing. Got that report from Harrison High?"

"You know you're off duty, don't you? You know they've sent someone down here to fill for you?"

"Oh yeah? Who?"

"Detective Sergeant Lorimer."

"Who the hell is that?"

"A probationer."

"And you are giving him orders?"

"Yes."

"Nine days on the job and you're in charge. Jesus."

"Mother always said that I fall on my feet."

Powder laughed. Then coughed.

"Guy's a loser, right?"

"I wouldn't say that," Fleetwood said.

"Because he's listening, right?"

"It's not appropriate to make snap decisions."

"That bad, eh?" Powder cackled to himself, but laughing hurt.

"The new man will be just fine when he gets the hang of your system," Fleetwood said. "Did you want something else?"

"I already asked for the news on Harrison High that you didn't give me."

Powder heard her saying, "Lorimer, take a look on that desk and bring me any telephone messages or reports." There was a pause. "No, that desk. There." Pause. "That is not a phone message." Pause. "Nothing?" She returned to Powder. "Nothing, Powder."

Powder laughed painfully. "The halt leading the blind," he said.

"You ought to rest," Fleetwood said.

"Got a hypothetical question for you."

He waited, but she was silent.

"Suppose I look into a guy's garage and see he's got bags of sand and cement."

"Yes . . . ?"

"And then I look in and they're not there."

"So?"

"What did he use them for?"

Fleetwood sighed.

"Well?"

"Concreting something," she said.

"Good work," he said genuinely.

"That's it?"

"That's it," Powder said. "And it means I am an idiot."

Powder browbeat a novice nurse into getting the note-book from his jacket, which was hanging in the room's closet. It had phone numbers and notes in it.

He called Ramey Fry, the manager of McCormick's Creek State Park's campsite.

Fry was markedly less interested in Powder's call than he had been on occasions before the dig.

Powder wanted to know if there was anybody on the site that William Weaver had occupied the previous weekend.

"Coming in this afternoon," Fry said.

"No, they're not," Powder said.

"What?"

"Keep them off. Give them another site."

"I couldn't do that," Fry said, sounding offended.

"I'm confiscating it. You'll get site rent payment for the trouble you go to relocating the new people, but they're not to use it."

"Why not?"

"Because we're digging again."

From Information, Powder got the number of the Owen County sheriff's office in Spencer. He expected more resistance than he encountered. But the sheriff was up for reelection in the fall. A speculative dig, if there was a chance for an interesting outcome, "as the result of information received," was welcomed.

"You'll need a crane," Powder told him.

"A what?"

"About two and a half feet down you're going to find cement. And if it is cement, instead of just rock, then I want it dug around and the whole thing lifted out. Can you supervise that for me?"

"Could take a couple of days," the sheriff said, but it wasn't by way of complaint.

Powder lay back on his bed. He started to rub his face. But didn't. Too much effort.

Instead he got up. Gritting his teeth at a certain amount of pain, he walked around the room. Then he found his pants in the closet and took some change out of the pocket.

He walked to the end of the hall where there was a coffee machine.

He was on his way back with a cup of coffee when he recognized a face. It was the head nurse on Jane Doe's ward.

They stopped and glared at each other.

The nurse said, "Just what do we think we are doing walking around the halls?" She took the coffee from him.

He didn't resist. He said, "I know how overworked you all are. I was just fending for myself for a minute or two."

"On my ward," the woman said, "you will fend for yourself if and when I say so. You got that?" She poked him on the bandages.

When he recovered, Powder said, "I got that."

After a rest he called the main branch of the public library, on St. Clair Street.

He found them very helpful. Yes, they would try to

find whether a William G. Weaver, Jr., had borrowed books on geological strata.

Then Powder called the Harrison High School assistant principal.

"Yes," he told her. "I *am* the cop you read about. I'm calling from my hospital bed. And my healing process is delayed because you didn't call me back yesterday with the information I wanted."

"I didn't get a chance to get into school until late in the afternoon," she said. "And then this morning I recognized the name . . ."

The assistant principal gave Powder an Indianapolis address for Sarah Crismore and also a "home" address, in Aurora, Indiana. With the qualification that a relationship was only rumor, she also provided the name and address of a male science teacher at the school.

Powder wrote them down in silence. And then asked, "Have you filled Crismore's job yet?"

"Well, no."

"If Sarah Crismore came to you soon, say by the end of the week, and asked to withdraw her resignation, would there be a chance of your reinstating her?"

"Lieutenant," the assistant principal said, "I don't quite understand where you fit in this."

"I asked you a pretty simple question," Powder said. "If you are assured that there is no question of outstanding police problems, what would your reaction be?"

"Of course," she began, "it's not by any means entirely my decision, but we would be likely to treat a request to withdraw an intemperate resignation sympathetically. Especially if there was some explanation about what had prompted it in the first place."

"I see. All right. Thank you."

* * *

Powder dozed before lunch, and awoke to find that his chest hurt more than it had in the morning.

When his lunch came, so did Ricky.

Ricky was aggrieved.

"I only found out what happened because I turned on the radio," he said.

"I don't think I have your new address on my next-of-kin card," Powder said.

"Hey, are you all right?"

"Great," Powder said.

"Come on," he insisted. "How *are* you?"

"Great. How's business?"

Ricky became immediately evasive. "Business?"

"It is a serious question," Powder said.

"Come on, Dad," Ricky said, irritated now. "Get off my back, will you?"

Powder inhaled, closing his eyes. "All right," he said.

Ricky said nothing.

"Go away now, will you? Let me eat in peace."

Ricky went away.

A doctor visited Powder's bedside shortly after the lunch dishes were cleared away.

"And how's the brave officer today?" the doctor asked.

"Irritable," Powder said.

"I see." The doctor, a chubby man with a carefully trimmed full beard, made a note.

"I want to know why I am being allowed to eat," Powder said.

"Oh?"

"General anesthesia requires fasting beforehand. If you're letting me eat, it seems to mean that you're not going in after the second slug yet. Why not?"

The doctor put down his clipboard.

"And spare me any posturing, will you. Just answer the question."

"The second bullet is awkwardly placed near your spine. We are hoping that leaving it for a while will see the bullet working itself back through the damaged tissue of the entry wound."

"A little bit is important, huh?"

"It could reduce the danger from operating very significantly."

"We're not talking about life-death danger, for the most part, are we?"

Looking Powder in the eyes, the doctor said, "Not for the most part, no."

"OK. When do you go in?"

"We won't wait for long. Probably you will be starved tonight against the chance of doing it tomorrow. We'll take another X ray in the morning. At most, we're likely to wait until day after tomorrow."

"I went for a little walk a couple of hours ago," Powder said.

"So I gather," the doctor said.

"Hurt a bit."

"I am sure it did," the doctor said.

When the doctor left, Powder rested. But he left his telephone on and within a quarter of an hour, it rang.

The librarian from the main branch reported that William Weaver had borrowed four books about general geology and Indiana geology. They had been taken out over a period from June to November of the previous year.

Powder thanked the librarian effusively and lay smiling at the ceiling.

The smile lasted several minutes. Then he made two calls.

The first was to Albert Samson. He got an answering machine. He told it, "I don't like these goddamn machines."

The second was to the Missing Persons office.

A sluggish male voice asked if he could help.

Powder resisted abuse. He asked for Fleetwood.

She was in.

"That was Lorimer?"

"Yes," she said.

"He sounds like he is underwater. Has he got a snorkel in his mouth?"

"What do you want, Powder? We're undermanned and there's a lot of work to do."

He said, "I had intended to tell you to sign off for tomorrow morning, but if you're so busy you better come around tonight, after work."

"Oh?"

"And don't bring me any fruit or stuff to eat. I won't be hungry."

29

*F*leetwood arrived just before six o'clock.

Powder appeared to be asleep, but as she closed the door his eyes opened, and he said, "My clothes are in the closet. Get them for me."

"No 'hello'?"

"We haven't got time."

Fleetwood hesitated, and then went to the closet. The hanging rail was too high for her to take the hangers from, but she tugged the clothes down.

When she brought them, Powder was sitting on the edge of the bed. After a moment of struggling, he asked her to help him with his trousers, socks, and shoes.

Finally he stood up.

Fleetwood said, "What am I doing? I've gotten into the habit of doing what you tell me and not even asking questions. I must be crazy."

"You'd make someone a wonderful old-fashioned wife," Powder said. "Come on. We may already be too late. They change shifts about now. You go ahead and hold the elevator. I'll get to it as fast as I can. They're not used to me in clothes. I should make it."

Fleetwood looked at him. "You sure you don't want a ride on my lap?"

"Cut the cackle, will you? I'm not up to it."

Powder made his escape without hitches.

In the main lobby, he told Fleetwood, "Bring your car around. I'll stand by the door looking lackadaisical and elegant."

Fleetwood brought the car to the front. It took her twenty minutes.

Powder slid into it slowly. Once settled he said, "I'm not going to complain about the time I had to wait," he said. "I understand and make allowance for your being a cripple." A spasm of pain came on him. She didn't notice it at first as she was working her way to the main road.

But she didn't ask if he wanted to go back. She said, "You mind telling me where we're heading?"

"Three Three Eight Wilmington Road."

"And just where is that?"

"In Aurora."

"What?"

"Aurora. It's a town near where Indiana borders Kentucky and Ohio. Follow the signs to Cincinnati on Interstate Seventy-four. We'll turn off at Greensburg, and go through Versailles. It may be a little farther, but it's more scenic."

After they cleared the Wanamaker exit of I-74, Powder asked Fleetwood to pull the car onto the berm.

When the car had stopped, he slouched in the passenger seat for a moment. Then he rubbed his face.

"I'm hungry," he said. "And I hurt."

She began to speak.

He interrupted. "But I can't have anything to eat or drink. I'm going to sleep for a while. That, at least, I can do. Just about anywhere, which is where I am. What I wanted to tell you was that you shouldn't worry, if I may be so presumptuous as to think you might have. I'll be all right when we get there."

He paused. Then he said, "That's where you kids waste so much of your energy."

"Where's that?"

"Feeling good when you don't have to. You worry if you don't feel great all the time. You get my age, you learn how to save up and feel good when you have to. OK. Let's get moving."

"It's your show," she said.

"Damn right," Powder said. He tried to shift in his seat, but it was hard.

He closed his eyes.

After about two hours of driving, Fleetwood prodded Powder's arm.

He didn't respond.

She prodded it again, and then she pulled over to the side of the road, killed the motor, and turned to the quiescent figure lying awkwardly in her passenger seat.

"Powder?"

With both hands, she shook his arm gently.

After a moment, the body came to life. He snapped himself into an attentive, upright position, as if responding to danger.

He looked around. Then the pain flooded in.

"Hey, take it easy, lady," he said. "I'm a sick man." Involuntarily he groaned. "Jesus," he said. "Medicine must be doing me good. Sure tastes bad."

"We're on the edge of Aurora."

"Sounds lovely," he said. "I hope this idea of yours works out. It's a long way to come on a wild-goose chase."

The address Powder had was of a small brick house with an immaculate front yard and a brilliant flower garden edging both the building and the large cement patio outside the front door. A cool breeze rustled the leaves of the neighborhood trees and through an arboreal gap the rippling upper Ohio River was plainly visible.

There was no sign of life from the front as Powder and Fleetwood paused to admire the view and the balmy evening. Then together they faced the patio, which was two steps above the path.

"You go on," Fleetwood said.

"Like hell." Powder turned her chair around. His full remaining strength, combined with her pull on the wheels, was just sufficient to get her up the two steps.

Powder leaned on the back of the chair, pale and too tired to speak.

After a couple of minutes' rest he knocked on the door with his fist.

After a few moments, the door was thrown open by a woman in her sixties. She was tiny, and her taut face was ringed with white curls.

She studied first Powder and then Fleetwood. "I don't subscribe to charities. And I don't buy at the door."

"Neither do we," Powder said.

"What do you want?" the woman asked.

"We are looking for Sarah, Mrs. Crismore," Powder said.

"My name ain't Crismore," the woman said.

"But you know who I mean."

"I do. Crismore. The name of her people. If you want to call them that." The woman narrowed her eyes. "You don't look like police, but you sound like 'em."

"We are police officers," Powder said, "although we are out of our jurisdiction. We'd like to come in for a few minutes."

Powder took his identification wallet from his pocket and opened it for the woman to examine. Taking his lead, Fleetwood did the same.

The woman studied them unhurriedly.

"Look all right," she said, as if convinced against her will. She stepped back. "Come on in then, if you have to."

In the living room an old man sat in an armchair that faced a side window of the house. After she seated Powder and Fleetwood, the woman went to the man and said, "Indianapolis police about the Crismore girl. Remember her?"

Without turning toward the visitors, the old man grunted dismissively.

"Name's Mayberry," the woman said, as she returned. She sat facing them. "Had a lot of children through here, over the years, my old man and me." She nodded toward the mantelpiece over the room's fireplace. More than twenty photographs of children stared individually out of dime-store frames.

"Orphans and rejects," Mrs. Mayberry continued. "County gives you a little money to bed and board them. Learn them standards and decency. Some pick it up and some don't."

She thought for a moment. "Sarah learned," she said, drawing her memory back. She rose and took a picture from the mantel. She studied the back of it. "Sarah was a good girl. Real quiet. Helpful," she said, as if doubtfully. "Why are the police after her?"

Fleetwood said, "We work in the Missing Persons Department. Sarah is missing."

"Oh dear," Mrs. Mayberry said without concern. She

studied the photograph again. "Always helping people and things. No, no real complaints about this one."

"How did she come to you?" Fleetwood asked.

"Father killed the rest of the family and himself. Left her. Nobody knew why. Maybe he lost count. There was seven kids. He got the other six."

Mrs. Mayberry put the picture back in its place. "Missing?" she asked. "It's happened before, you know."

"When?" Powder asked.

"Child broke its neck once. Fell out'n a tree. Eighteen years old and climbing trees. Spotted some broke-winged bird. Five months in bed. The high school graduated her anyhow and a college near here saw about her in the paper and give her a scholarship to be a teacher. Stupid work for a quiet child, I say. But she wouldn't have gone to college otherwise. Still, time come for her to go and she wandered off. Found her next day in the woods. But I suppose that's not the same kind of thing you're working on."

"No," Fleetwood said.

"When did you last hear from her?" Powder asked.

"Had a card said she got work in Indianapolis. Last summer. Never really thought she'd make the grade." Mrs. Mayberry shrugged. "But I'm sometimes wrong."

30

*P*owder was silent for several miles. He held his head.

"Hurting?" Fleetwood sked.

"Only for a grown-up kid who thinks she's bad when it's really everybody else."

Fleetwood said nothing.

"I'm a bit numb," Powder said. Then, "If it weren't summer vacation, I'd say we should head to Madison. Where she went to college. Maybe you can get someone to answer the phone there tomorrow."

"So, what now?"

"Wake me when we get to the city limits."

Fifteen minutes later, Powder roused himself to say, slurrily, "Put the radio on. It won't bother me."

About twenty miles from downtown Indianapolis, Powder sat up and asked, clearly, "Why do you need so badly to stay a cop?"

Fleetwood was caught in a fifty-five-mile-per-hour reverie. "What?"

Powder repeated the question word for word and added, "It's an obsession with you. What's wrong with not being a cop? I don't understand."

"I don't know what to say to you."

"Just answer the question. I want to know."

Fleetwood spoke slowly. "I remember the times when I was on the street, or entering buildings, or waiting ..." Her voice drifted away. Powder turned the radio off.

"I remember times," she said, "when to stay alive I had to be aware of everything going on around me because something in a window, or a noise behind, some little thing ... if I missed it, I might be dead."

Powder listened while she was silent.

"And at times like that," Fleetwood said, "I felt more alive than any other times in my life."

When they got inside the bypass loop around the city, Powder said, "We're not going back to the hospital yet."

Fleetwood looked at him.

She said, "Where to?"

Powder gave her the address on Tacoma that had been the listed address of Sarah Crismore.

"She's not in the hospital," Powder said. "She's not in Aurora. She's got to be somewhere."

"How about you telling me something, Powder?"

"Maybe."

"You were half-dead when we started this jaunt and you're worse now. Why the urgency about finding this woman?"

"I need to have it settled. At least up to a point."

"Won't it keep?"

Powder was quiet for a moment before he said, "No."

They approached the address in silence, a modern brick apartment building with two dozen units.

Posted on the wall next to the mailboxes was a telephone number for inquiries. But Powder buzzed number 1 instead.

A fat woman in a heavy brown dress came into the lobby and asked Powder through the glass who he was.

Powder showed his police identification. The woman let him and Fleetwood in. He said, "There must be someone on the premises with spare keys to the apartments in the building. Do you know who it is?"

"I do," the woman said in a resonant voice.

"Who is it, please?"

"Me," the woman said. "You got a warrant?"

"No," Powder said. He looked the woman in the eyes.

She stared back at him for a moment. Then chuckled. "Ask a silly question," she said. "Which one you want?"

"I don't know the number. But it was recently vacated by a woman in her twenties, who lived alone."

"Oh yeah," the woman said dismissively, "the teacher. Number eleven. One floor up." The woman disappeared for a moment and reappeared with a key. Then she frowned. "What's there goes with the place. She cleared her own stuff out."

Powder nodded wearily. "Thanks."

"You want me to come up?"

"No," Powder said.

"OK," the woman said. She made a point of looking past Powder to Fleetwood's wheelchair. She shrugged and retreated to her apartment.

Powder turned to Fleetwood. "Go in and talk to her."

"What about?"

"I don't know," he said irritably. "When she last saw Sarah Crismore or ... anything. I don't care. Just do it."

Fleetwood looked at him, puzzled and even hurt.

"Because I don't want you watching me try to climb these stairs. All right?"

Powder spent only a few minutes in the apartment. It was minimally furnished, but clearly unoccupied. No sheets on the bed, no food in the cabinets, no personal papers.

No occupant.

He knocked on the door of number 1 when he got back down.

Fleetwood thanked the heavy woman in the brown dress for her cooperation and Powder returned the apartment key.

When they were in the car Fleetwood said, "Sarah Crismore hasn't been back since she cleared out."

"Surprise, surprise."

"But there are some letters for her."

Powder squinted and turned to Fleetwood.

"She gave them to me," Fleetwood said. She passed them over, and turned on the internal car light.

Powder flipped through the five envelopes. Three were of commercial origin. Two appeared to be letters, one postmarked in Indianapolis and one that had been hand-delivered.

Powder snorted and put them in his lap. He turned the light out.

Fleetwood said, "She didn't leave a forwarding address."

Powder was still silent.

"You're not going to open them?" Fleetwood asked.

"And commit a federal crime?"

"Well, what now?" Fleetwood asked.

"What now? What now? Goddamned broken record," Powder snapped.

They sat for a few moments.

Fleetwood almost asked if he was in pain.

Powder, with eyes closed, said, "She's got to be somewhere, right?"

"Right."

"So, how to track her." It was a statement.

He was taking short breaths.

After several moments Powder said, "What did she wear when she left the hospital? No clothes coming in. What did she wear going out? What's she wearing now?"

"As far as they know, she walked out in hospital pajamas."

"The kind with the ties at the back?" Powder asked. "No. Either she pinched some or she called someone to come to her, bring things, pick her up."

"Do you know what time it is?" the man asked at the door.

"Time I was in bed," Powder said. He held up his identification.

"What's that?" The man looked at the ID. "Police?"

"Are you Paul Kanouse?"

"Yes. Are you really a policeman?"

"I am," Powder said.

"Well, what do you want?"

"I want Sarah Crismore, Mr. Kanouse."

The man went rigid.

A voice from inside the house asked, "Who is it? Paul, who is it?"

Kanouse called to the voice, "Just Ken, wanting help pushing his car to a start. I'll be back in a few minutes."

Kanouse joined Powder on the front porch and closed the door behind him.

Powder said, "I was going to ask you to come out to my car anyway. My colleague is waiting for us there."

They joined Fleetwood, and sat in the vehicle in front of the house.

"I think," Powder told her, "that Mr. Kanouse knows where Sarah Crismore is."

"Has Sarah done something wrong? Has she committed some crime?" Kanouse asked.

Powder rubbed his face.

"You know where she is, yes?"

Kanouse hesitated.

"And you helped her get out of County Hospital. What did she do, call you?"

Kanouse looked increasingly frightened. "I don't know how you knew about me."

"You were her lover, weren't you?"

"I hadn't seen her for weeks," he protested. "I didn't know where she was or what had happened to her. Out of the blue she called me to meet her at the hospital with some clothes."

"Which you did."

"Yeah," he said.

"And what then?"

"I found her . . . a place to stay."

"Where?"

"I . . . don't want to tell you. She doesn't want people to know."

Powder was silent for a moment. Then said, "All right."

Kanouse was as surprised as Fleetwood was.

Powder said, "How is she?"

"OK."

"She didn't tell you what she was in hospital for?"

"No," Kanouse said. "I saw her face. . . . I didn't ask."

"You've seen her today?"

Lowering his voice, Kanouse said, "Well, sure."

"And what does she say about the future?"

"Just that she'll be out of my hair in a few days."

"How exactly?"

Kanouse seemed surprised by the question. "I don't know. I've loaned her a little money. I think she's going someplace. To her stepparents, maybe. I don't think she has any other family."

"And how do you feel about that?"

"What?"

"Her being out of your hair."

"Not too long ago I would have begged her to stay."

"But . . . ?"

"She seemed to . . . go funny. And she dumped me."

"Is she still funny?"

"There's something not quite right." He sighed with some feeling. "Always did seem too good to be true."

Kanouse's front door opened and the silhouette of a tall, angular woman appeared in the frame. She looked around and slammed the door.

"I must seem like a bastard to you," Kanouse said quietly. "But it's not working out." He gestured to his house. "With her. And there are no kids. And there is part of me that really loves teaching. I get a charge, you know, when I can get a kid that other teachers have written off to sit up and pay attention to something. Sarah shares that with me. In there," he nodded to his house, "it's push, push, push for advancement and standard of living."

Powder said, "We are stricken to hear about your difficulties."

He took the five envelopes addressed to Sarah Crismore. He threw them into Kanouse's lap. "Deliver those to Miss Crismore tomorrow for us, please."

Kanouse fingered the envelopes. "Yeah. Sure."

"And tell her that her job at the school is probably still open for her."

"It is?" Kanouse asked.

"Tell her to get in touch with me, or my colleague."

"All right."

Powder grabbed the man's arm forcefully. "Make sure you do."

*   *   *

When Kanouse had left the car, Powder said, "Just one more stop."

"You look terrible."

"I wouldn't be healthy if I didn't."

Fleetwood said, "You could have made him tell you where she was. Just by asking one more time."

"Sure," Powder said. He closed his eyes.

"So why didn't you?"

"I've got a way of contacting her now," he said. "And if she's not hiding, then she'll be in touch with us."

"And if she is still hiding?"

"Suppose he tells her that we know where she is. What would she do but pack up and go someplace else? I don't want that. I'm kind of tired of wandering around the countryside."

"Mmmmm."

"So let's get a move on, huh?"

The stop was at the office of Albert Samson. In the comparative darkness of a residential area, Samson's neon sign seemed out of place. And its Christmasy reflections off the high barb-topped fence made the detective's premises seem out of season as well.

Powder got out of the car and banged on the front door.

After a minute, a light showed inside and the door opened. Samson recognized Powder. Surprised, he said, "You were shot. I was going to visit you. Bring you some flowers."

"I've saved you the trouble."

Fleetwood appeared and Powder said, "Let us in."

"I want you to do something for me," Powder said.

"I have been, all day," Samson said lightly. "Tailing your crook son."

Powder hesitated only a moment. "Well, now I want you to follow someone else. A guy who's going to lead you to a lady."

Samson recognized the degree of difficulty with which Powder was speaking. He nodded. "Let's have it."

At the hospital, Powder sought to reassure the night nurse by informing her that he had had more than three hours sleep while he was out. Fleetwood began to confirm what he said, but her presence seemed only to anger the nurse. She shook her head furiously. "A man in your condition. I am not impressed," she said sternly. "If you were trying to impress me, you have failed completely."

Powder rubbed his face.

"You get to bed immediately."

Powder said, "If I didn't hurt so much, I would laugh."

31

X rays showed the bullet had moved more than two inches.

Powder felt puffed up through the middle and even achier than the day before. It was just as well he was fasting; he didn't feel hungry.

The doctor greeted him somberly early in the morning to talk about the X rays.

Powder asked, "The bullet going to move more?"

"I wouldn't have thought so. I've never known one to move this far, although I understand you had a more active day yesterday than was planned."

"The police athletics day comes up in a few weeks and I'm training for the hundred."

"Do you know what you risked?"

"No," Powder said. "And please don't tell me."

The doctor looked at the film again. "I think we should go in and get it today," he said.

"Can it be done with a local anesthetic?" Powder asked.

The medical eyebrows came up momentarily.

"I like to watch if guys poke around in me. Makes them more careful."

"Oh yes?"

Powder said, "If I don't go out completely, I'll be mentally together more quickly, won't I?"

"Not necessarily. What is it that so urgently needs your attention?"

Powder shrugged. "There are things I want to keep track of."

"Do you know how lucky you were with the path of this wound?"

"I live a charmed life," Powder said.

The doctor looked at his watch. "We'll probably go in early this afternoon."

When the doctor left, Powder took the telephone and called Missing Persons.

A male voice answered. Powder said, "Lorimer?"

"Yeah, that's right," the voice said.

"Is anybody else there? Sergeant Fleetwood or Agnes Shorter?"

"Uh, no. Not Lieutenant Powder, neither. He's in hospital, all shot up."

"This *is* Powder," Powder said.

"Oh. Gee. How you doing, Lieutenant?"

"I want to know whether there are any messages for me."

"Gee! Ain't that something! I only just took two calls for you in the last few minutes."

Powder waited.

Lorimer asked, "Do you want to know what they were?"

"Of course I goddamned want to know what they were!"

"Oh," Lorimer said, "all right. The first one was from Sergeant Bull. He said to tell you that someone called Marianna Gilkis has turned up in St. Paul with her boyfriend."

Lorimer hesitated.

Powder said, "What was the other one?"

"That was weird. From a woman. Funny damn message, but maybe it'll mean something to you."

"Get on with it!"

"Exactly what she said was 'He passed me on. The bastard passed me on.' Her word, Lieutenant. I don't much care for bad language in a woman, myself."

"Is that all she said?"

"Yeah. I asked who it was, but she didn't say nothing to that. And she sounded hell's upset that you weren't here. Must not of read the papers or watched the TV, huh? Pretty famous guy you are now."

"Has Fleetwood checked in there yet today?"

"No," Fleetwood said from the doorway of Powder's room.

"Uh, no, she hasn't, I don't think," Lorimer said on the telephone.

"Any other messages for me?"

"Shall I look on your desk?"

"Look on my desk."

While he waited, Powder said to Fleetwood, "Come in, come in. Don't sit there like your battery was dead."

Fleetwood rolled in.

"You look terrible," Powder said.

"What's that?" Lorimer asked.

"I said you look terrible, Lorimer. Must be the strain of the new assignment."

Doubtfully Lorimer said, "Well, they said it was only for a while."

"Messages," Powder said.

"No. Nothing else I can see."

"Terrific work, Lorimer. Keep it up, kid."

"Uh, right. Thanks."

Powder turned to Fleetwood. "You really do look awful," he said.

"I had a late night," Fleetwood said. "Followed by an early morning."

"There's room in here," Powder said, patting his bed. "Take a load off your seat."

"It's a real tempting offer," Fleetwood said heavily. "So how did you do?"

"She's at the Forrest, a hotel in town. Kanouse went out to her a little after eight."

Powder nodded slowly. "Samson still there?"

"Yes. Awaiting further instructions. But if she leaves, he'll follow her."

"Is the Forrest the one on North Street?"

"Yes."

"Samson's where? In the lobby?"

"That's where I left him."

Powder nodded. "OK. Good."

Fleetwood cocked her head.

"Go on," Powder said. "Give poor old Lorimer a hand."

Powder was on the edge of his bed when Lieutenant Gaulden appeared.

"What an honor," Powder said.

"We were all terribly upset to hear what happened."

"I wouldn't upset you for the world," Powder said.

"I'm glad to see you sitting up. I gather you've got an operation later on today."

"Yeah."

"I also wanted to assure you that we were putting in temporary cover at the office and that things are in hand."

"I've talked to Lorimer," Powder said.

"You've talked to him?"

"I was thinking of skipping the operation and dropping into the office this afternoon to help him out. All the work goes through there is a little too much for him."

"I don't understand your concern," Gaulden said sharply. "Chief Snyder said you were talking about taking retirement."

"Ahhhh," Powder said.

"I don't want you to pack it in any more than he does," Gaulden said, "but I can understand your feelings. You've got more than enough time in for full pension. Nice little payoff in a lump sum to get you on your way. More than most because you have a stack of unused leave time. I can understand you'd be thinking about it seriously at a time like this. You'd have to be."

"I suppose you've brought the appropriate forms," Powder said.

"I only know what Snyder said to me," Gaulden said defensively. "He seemed to think that you were pretty positive. And we all know what a determined man you are, once you get your mind made up about something."

"Leave them on my bedside table," Powder said. "I'll read them later on."

"I don't want you to misinterpret this," Gaulden said, as he pulled four sheets of paper out of his briefcase.

"There is no chance of my doing that," Powder said.

When Gaulden left, Powder rested by calling the sheriff of Owen County.

"I was just about to phone you," the sheriff told Powder.

Powder was unconvinced.

The sheriff continued, "I've been coordinating with the local press and photo boys. And it's only just about finished."

"What exactly were you going to call me about?" Powder asked.

"Why, last night we found that lump of cement! Just like you said."

"Did you now?"

"That's right."

"And what is inside it?"

"Well, we haven't broke it open just yet. We've lifted it out whole this morning and the breaking will be supervised by the county coroner."

"I'd be pleased to hear your results."

"Course you would. And I'll call you right away."

"OK. I'll be out for an hour or two. But anytime after that."

Powder rested five more minutes. Then he heaved himself back to a sitting position. He dropped his legs over the edge of the bed and slid until his feet touched the floor.

There he waited for a slight dizziness to pass.

He got up from the bed and went to the closet where his clothes had been put, again.

The hardest were his shoes and socks. In the end he didn't tie his shoes, just tucking the laces in the sides

32

*F*rom outside, the Forrest Hotel looked like a small brick office building. Unlike several marginal downtown hotels, there was nothing in its architecture or decor to suggest that it had ever seen better times.

Albert Samson was lounging in the lobby in a suit that made him look inconspicuous. He saw Powder enter and immediately rose and came to him.

"What are you doing here?" Samson asked.

"What room is she in?"

"Three oh one."

"I've come to cover till a relief man gets here," Powder said. "There's something important that you have to do."

"And my granny plays for the Pacers," Samson said.

"Cut the crap," Powder said, mustering forcefulness. "Listen. A kid called Harold Sillit was shot and killed a couple of weeks ago. He had a friend. Someone he'd share special secrets with. I need to know who and where he is. I need it now. Fleetwood will help. She's at the office."

Samson looked dubious.

"Move, damn it!" Powder shouted.

Samson went.

Powder shuffled to the hotel desk. His progress was watched by a knobbly man of about sixty. The man's voice, however, was rich and low. He said, "What can I do for you, mister?"

Powder showed the man his identification card.

Looking from the ID to Powder back to the ID, the man said, "Old picture, huh?"

"There's a woman in 301."

"So?"

"Is she alone?"

"How do I know?"

Irritably, Powder said, "You know whether the guy who checked her in is here."

"He left," the man said.

"And you know whether anybody besides the man I just talked to has asked for her room number."

The hotel man narrowed his eyes. He said, "The PI gave me ten bucks for my help."

Powder snarled. "Has anybody else asked for her room?"

"Nobody," the man said.

"All right. Now, where's the elevator?" For a moment he was afraid the place wouldn't have one, not knowing if he could make it to the third floor.

"Through there, on the left," the man said.

When he got out, Powder looked for directions to 301.

He had to guess. He went left, and it was the first door he came to. His lucky day.

When he knocked a voice from inside said immediately, "Come in." A woman's voice.

Powder tried the handle. He walked into the room.

In front of him, spread on top of the bed, was Sarah Crismore.

She was naked, save for a gun in her hand.

Powder rubbed his face.

Crismore was not apparently agitated. She trained the

gun's barrel on Powder. "What do *you* want?"

"What are you offering?" Powder asked, trying to find his 'right guy' light tone of voice. He looked for a table to lean on, feeling faint, but there was none high enough to help him.

"I offer death and destruction," Crismore said.

"That's nice. For anybody in particular, or do I get to play too?"

"You do if you try to stop me," the woman said.

"Stop you? Why should I try to stop you? I'm already over the legal limit for lead in the system."

She said nothing. The direction of the gun did not vary.

"I take it this has something to do with the message you left for me?"

"Message?" Her eyes were questioning.

"At headquarters. You left a message for me a few hours ago."

"Oh . . . yes." Vaguely.

"Something about being passed on. I take it the late unlamented Harold Sillit mentioned his escapade to a friend."

Her lips drew taut.

The rest of her body grew tense.

The gun fired.

It surprised them both.

Powder didn't feel the wind of the bullet, but a hole in the wall behind him showed that it must have passed close.

The recoil lifted the gun toward the ceiling for the moment. When Crismore let it drop again, it went all the way to her thigh.

But it jerked up again. "Oh, it's hot!" she said.

"Off to the side, please," Powder said, waving his hand.

She lowered the gun to the bedspread. But she kept a grip, and her finger was still on the trigger.

"Where did you get this one?" Powder asked of the gun.

"It's Paul's," she said.

"Helpful, sensitive guy," Powder said.

Crismore watched him.

"How do you know you were 'passed on'?" he asked.

"Note in the mailbox."

"That one without a stamp?"

"Yes."

"What did it say?"

"It said, 'Harold told me all about you, and I want some too. Don't think you can get away. I'll spread it all around if you try, so better tell me where you are. Get your cunt ready. Edward.' " She recited the message as if it were a school exercise. And then she said, "It was a dirty, scrawly, scratchy scribble on a torn-off piece of paper."

"From some friend of Sillit's?"

"His brother."

Powder rubbed his face again. He felt tired. "So," he said gesturing to her, "what's all this?"

Crismore said, "The kid says be ready. I'm ready."

"He's coming here?"

"I suppose so."

"How does he know you're here?"

"He said to tell him where I am. I told him where I am. I gave Paul a message to deliver on his way back to his wife."

"And just what kind of reception party are you planning?"

Heavily, she said, "Harold was evil. His brother is evil. I've learned my lesson. There's only one thing you can do with evil."

She lifted the gun from the bed and pointed it at Powder. She closed one eye. She aimed, and said, "Pow!"

"All this because you made one mistake?" he asked.

"What mistake?" Airy, seemingly unconcerned.

"Failing to protect yourself that first time." No reaction. Powder said, "Fine, you grew up not knowing how to recognize the bad guys. And not knowing how they spot the weak, and use the weak. But it's *not* too late. It's not a hole you can't get out of. You can get your life back. You can."

"Oh yes? How's that?"

"The first thing to do is to give me that gun."

She didn't have time for due consideration.

Behind Powder, the hotel room door opened, and a large, smirking, pimply boy bounded in, saw the naked woman on the bed, and allowed himself a broad smile.

Crismore re-aimed the gun and shot the leering child. He fell back, in shock, against the wall.

Powder moved to get between the boy and the gun. But he didn't have the speed.

Crismore shot the sitting figure twice more.

Powder turned, instead, toward the bed.

As he approached Crismore stuck the short pistol barrel in her own mouth.

But involuntarily she jerked it out.

"Hot," she said. "Smelly."

By the time she realized Powder was close, and moved to overcome her fastidiousness, he had grabbed the weapon and pulled it from her.

In his fury, Powder hurled the weapon through the hotel room's window.

The effort cost him his balance, and he fell beside the bed.

He didn't even try to get up.

He pulled the room telephone by its wire. It crashed to the floor. He told the desk clerk to get the police and an ambulance.

Near him, Sarah Crismore lay on the bed, holding herself.

33

*T*he operation was done in the early evening and the bullet near Powder's spine was removed without apparent complications.

Powder was unconscious for several hours and then drowsy for several more. He remembered only snatches of thoughts when he surfaced late the next morning.

He remembered a vision of his garden, overgrown, jungly with large fruits. And of walking around his apartment looking for his mother.

Powder woke up with the sun shining through net curtains.

He decided he felt good.

He tried to sit up; he decided he felt bad.

He dozed again. He dreamed, or thought, about William G. Weaver, Jr. He woke up saying, "Dig. Dig!"

"What?"

"Who's that?" Powder asked.

"Open your eyes and look," Fleetwood said.

Powder blinked his eyes a few times. Then closed them. "Too much trouble," he said.

Fleetwood watched him for a moment.

Then she locked the wheels of her chair and swung her legs to the floor between chair and bed. She raised herself and balanced on her feet. Using one hand on the chair and one hand on the bed frame above Powder's head, she stooped and kissed him lightly on the forehead.

Powder said, "I felt that. And don't think I can't tell the difference between lips and two wet fingers."

He looked at her. Tears welled in his eyes. He held them back. He thought of Sarah Crismore and he turned away. "It all went too fast for me."

"You feel as bad as you look?" Fleetwood asked.

After a moment, Powder said, "What day is it? How long have I been out? When did I talk to you last?"

"It's tomorrow. I talked to you yesterday."

He turned to her. "Do something for me, will you?"

"What's that?"

"Go bust William Weaver."

"Come on, give it a rest, Powder."

He struggled to sit. The movement hurt again. He groaned.

"In my notebook, there's a number for the sheriff of Owen County. He'll explain. Then go bust the bastard."

Fleetwood said nothing.

Powder said, "What's your problem?"

Fleetwood said, "I already spoke to the sheriff. He called you.'"

"And?"

"There was nothing in the cement."

"What?"

"They grappled the lump out and the coroner cracked it open with hammer and chisel. Local photographer standing by. There was nothing inside, and the sheriff is hot enough to cook an egg on."

"Nothing," Powder repeated, absorbing.

"Look," Fleetwood said, now irritated. "Just how alert are you?"

"I'm fine," Powder said.

"Your head is clear?"

"Spit it out," he said.

"I also talked to the private detective, Samson."

"Oh?"

"And he told me you've had him tailing your son."

"Did he now? And did he give you a typed report in triplicate too?"

"He said you are looking for evidence that the kid is doing illegal things and that there are plenty of indications the evidence is there."

"I see," Powder said coldly.

"I just want to say to you, Powder, leave it alone."

Powder said nothing.

"Be guided by me on this," Fleetwood said feelingly. "You can't replace family. Warn the kid off again. Threaten him. But don't push it."

"I only have one thing to say on this subject."

"Yeah?"

"It's for you to tell your new chum that he's off the job. Tell him to send me his bill."

"I shouldn't have said anything. You aren't up to it." She rolled to the door.

"Wait a minute, Sergeant," Powder said.

She turned.

"What you going to do about William G. Weaver, Junior?"

Fleetwood looked at him.

"Be guided by me on this," he said. "Number one. The hole in McCormick's Creek State Park."

"What about it?"

"People don't pour cement into holes in the ground for nothing. It's not that kind of fun."

Fleetwood blinked.

"If there's nothing in the cement, there must be something under it. Tell the sheriff to get his photographer and a shovel."

Fleetwood remained silent.

"Number two."

"Yeah?"

"People don't move roses this time of year."

"What?"

"Plant them if they are in containers, fine. But not established bushes."

"What the hell are you saying?"

"I remembered this morning. When I saw the bastard last, he was transplanting roses. So, get yourself a warrant, and your own shovel, and go out to his garden . . ."

"No photographer?" Fleetwood asked.

About noon a nurse came to offer Powder something to drink.

"How about some eats?" he asked.

"We don't feed people who have been under general anesthesia for twenty-four hours. In case of complications."

"No complications with me," Powder said. "I'm very, very simple."

Around one, Albert Samson arrived.

"Do me a favor, will you, Samson?"

"What's that?"

"Ask the nurses out there if they like fresh fruit and vegetables."

Samson jumped up. "Sure, Leroy. Don't know why I didn't think of it myself."

But instead of going to the door he approached Powder's bedside and dropped an envelope on the patient's stomach. "Have a look at that while I'm gone."

Samson was out of the room for a quarter of an hour and Powder read through the surveillance report on Ricky.

The most damning direct observations confirmed what Powder felt he already knew. Part of this confirmation came from Ricky's visits to a number of sites at which he could well have been servicing long-standing telephone tap equipment. Samson provided locations and photographs, so finding the recording apparatus, if it was there, would be easy.

In addition, Samson established Ricky's direct association with Commercial Investigations. At the end of the site visits, Ricky had gone into CI with a package. The speculation was that he was delivering tapes.

What Powder hadn't already known was Commercial Investigations' history and reputation. Samson spelled this out, describing CI's origins as a legitimate investigative company nearly felled by a lawsuit in 1975. This had precipitated a change in the controlling hands and philosophy of the company. "Their reputation now," Samson wrote, "is wrong-side-of-the-fence. They concentrate on the backdoor and pressure trading of commercial information that straight outfits won't touch. With a hint of rough and tumble. They've grown fast in the last few years and they've picked up a lot of ex-cops, because they're easy to get licenses for. Doesn't matter if they left the force because of violence problems or other flaws. As a detective agency they do some legit work, but their big 'strength' is all the contacts they have with people looking for a few fast bucks, like your kid. Even among private detectives they're considered a blot on the landscape. It's felt they've been lucky that your esteemed trade hasn't caught up with them already."

A final observation was that Ricky had met two people briefly in public places. "To me, they looked like meets to pass goods. Too open to be drugs. But given the rep of CI, I'd have to surmise they were passing information or objects for CI to sell or use." Samson included photographs of the two people Ricky had met. They were Dwayne Grove and Lila Lee.

Powder read the report a second time.

Then he set it on his bedside table and rubbed his face.

For raising enough serious suspicion to open a case, it was more than sufficient.

Samson came back carrying a cup of vending machine coffee.

"How'd you get on?" he asked. "Or are your lips still moving and your fingers still running over the pages line by line?"

"It's not all there," Powder said.

"What do you mean?"

"No bill."

"Forget it."

"Like hell I'll forget it."

"I'll send it to you."

"You'll work it out for me here and now," Powder said.

The surgeon who had operated on Powder came around in the midafternoon. He did a phony double take as he walked into the room.

"With your recent history," the doctor said, "I'm surprised to find that you haven't checked out to go for a drive around the Five Hundred track before dinner."

Powder heard about the "pit murder" on the television at six o'clock. The news report showed the sheriff of Owen County speaking enthusiastically about his department's efficient persistence in following up "information received" to recover a woman's body buried in a "pit" in the nearby state park.

Fifteen minutes later Fleetwood called.

"I see you learned how to use the telephone," Powder said.

Sounding puzzled, Fleetwood said, "I have some news."

"They found the body; I know."

"You know?"

"Sure."

"How?"

"I saw it on the news."

Fleetwood sounded confused. "The news? You mean TV?"

"Of course I mean TV."

"I didn't see any cameras or reporters around."

Powder hesitated. "You didn't see . . . ? What do you mean?"

"I've been here all afternoon, and I didn't see any TV people at all. I'm surprised they knew about it. Much less got a report out."

"Where are you?" Powder asked.

"At Weaver's house," Fleetwood said. "Where else?"

"And what body are you talking about?"

"Annie Weaver's, under the goddamn rosebushes, of course."

34

*F*leetwood appeared at the hospital at quarter to nine that evening. She entered Powder's room and rolled to the edge of his bed without saying anything. He watched as she pulled a collection of papers from a bag.

"I've come from the office," she said. "Thought you might want the messages in your box, since I was coming anyway."

"You look terrible. Have you ever considered getting yourself shot? It's a great rest cure."

She was too tired to respond.

"What's the matter? No sense of humor? Well, better get on with it. As briefly as you can manage."

"There's not a lot to say."

"So, tell me about the bodies."

"Mrs. Weaver, and a lady friend."

Powder looked at her, puzzled, "Friend?"

"Friend, as in 'lover.' "

Powder shook his head in disbelief. "Sergeant Fleetwood strikes again," he said.

Fleetwood rubbed her face with both hands.

Of many questions he might have asked, Powder chose "Why did he bury them in different places?"

"He was going to put them both at McCormick's Creek. But in the end, he only put the friend there."

Powder waited.

"What he said to me was that he had gotten used to having Annie around the house."

Before she left, Powder asked Fleetwood to stop back at eleven in the morning. "And sleep late," he told her. It was by way of an order.

After she left, he read through the papers she had brought him. The messages that Lorimer had said weren't on his desk. Not on the desk but in his pigeonhole. Powder fumed at the incompetence.

There was a memo from Sergeant Bull. It said that Clive Burrus had been interrogated, eliminated, and released. The presumption now about the burned body was that it was that of a prostitute who had died unexpectedly but naturally among people whose concern for their own convenience far surpassed any worry about the niceties of law or respect for the dead. Bull was working with Vice Branch. There were no hard leads.

With Bull's memo there was a copy of the arrest report on Sarah Crismore. She was being confined for observation.

There was also a note from Tidmarsh in Computers to say that a more detailed and complete effort to establish a statistically significant relationship between the disappearances from centers of travel showed that no connection between the events was indicated. Agnes was, however, being retained on assignment with the central computer section. A replacement part-time secretary would be appointed.

Then Powder read through the resignation documents Gaulden had left for him to sign. He did not reread Samson's report on Ricky.

* * *

When a nurse brought him sleeping pills, Powder cajoled her into going for an envelope and stamps. But when she brought them, he put off his decision and took the pills.

Once he had eaten breakfast, Powder delayed no longer. He picked up the telephone and called Lieutenant Gaulden.

Gaulden said, "Ahhh, Lieutenant Powder."

"I've read through the resignation documents you left," Powder said.

"Yes?"

"If I go, will Fleetwood take over in Missing Persons?"

Gaulden measured his words. "You know I am not in a position to promise anything on my own, but I'm sure that the appointments board would look most carefully at any recommendations you might make."

"Thanks a lot," Powder said.

"Oh. Is that all?"

"I would appreciate it if you could come to my room here at eleven."

"Well, I'm not sure . . ."

"I want to settle my future formally."

"Certainly. Of course. I'll be there."

"Be on time," Powder said.

"Naturally," Gaulden said with the cool politeness of a generous victor.

When he was off the phone, Powder lay back on his bed feeling the will to fight back pulse painfully through his body. The audacity of the likes of Gaulden trying to pass him off with bureaucratic mush.

Powder found that he could not contain himself. He sat up, tore the resignation papers in half, and dropped them in the wastebasket. Only then did he begin to feel calm.

He took the envelope he'd obtained the previous night

and addressed it to Sergeant Bull. Into it he put Samson's report on Ricky. He rang for a nurse. When she came he asked her to mail it. It's what a cop had to do. And he couldn't stop being a cop.

It turned out to be the only line he knew how to take.

Finally, Powder called Ben Brown, the *Star*'s police reporter.

"What can I do for you, Lieutenant Powder?" Brown asked cautiously.

"I hope I can do something for you," Powder said genially.

"Oh yes?"

"You know all about the astonishing successes the Missing Persons Department has had since Carollee Fleetwood was assigned to us."

"Yeah ..."

"Well, what's happened only shows what Missing Persons could do if we got more quality officers and if our help for the distressed public was made a higher priority."

"Yeah ..."

"So I'm holding a press conference. At eleven in my hospital room. Sergeant Fleetwood will be here and available for interview. And a representative from the manpower side of the department's administration will be here to comment on my plans. I think it will make you a good story."

"You may be right," Brown said.

"And bring a photographer," Powder said. "Fleetwood always takes a nice picture and the more good PR we can get, the better."